ID0960548

Geronimo Stilton

THE VOLCANO OF FIRE

THE FIFTH ADVENTURE IN THE KINGDOM OF FANTASY

Scholastic Inc.

Library of Congress Cataloging-in-Publication data available.

ISBN 978-0-545-55625-5

Based on an original idea by Elisabetta Dami.

www.geronimostilton.com

Published by Scholastic Inc., 557 Broadway, New York, NY 10012. SCHOLASTIC and associated logos are trademarks and/or registered trademarks of Scholastic Inc.

Text by Geronimo Stilton
Original title *Quinto viaggio nel Regno della Fantasia*
Cover by Danilo Barozzi
Illustrations by Danilo Barozzi (design), Silvia Bigolin (design), Gabo Leon Bernstein (design and color), Christian Aliprandi (color) and Piemme's Archives
Graphics by Marta Lorini

Special thanks to Kathryn Cristaldi
Translated by Julia Heim
Interior design by Kay Petronio

14 13 12 11 10   17 18 19 20 21/0

Printed in China   38

First printing, September 2013

Geronimo Stilton

I am a bestselling author and publisher of *The Rodent's Gazette,* the most famouse newspaper on Mouse Island. This is my fifth trip to the **KINGDOM OF FANTASY**.

King Thunderhorn

I am the King of the Elves. Not long ago, Cackle put a spell on me and turned me into a white deer. Thanks to Geronimo, I am now back to being an elf.

Emerald

I am King Thunderhorn's sister, and Princess of the Elves. I may be younger than my brother, but I'm just as tough and courageous!

Sterling

I am the Princess of the Silver Dragons. I'm not afraid to go into battle, and I know all the tricks to tame a dragon!

Professor Longwind

I am the chancellor of the Great Explanatorium, the place where all of the smartest scientists in the Kingdom of Fantasy live.

First Volume (Vol)

I am a talking book at the Great Explanatorium. I am the first of twelve volumes of an encyclopedia, but my dream is to one day become an exciting adventure book.

Sproutness

I am the Princess of the Kingdom of the Fairies, and the Fairy of the Earth. My sister is Blossom, Queen of the Fairies. I can make seedlings sprout to life.

ANOTHER CRAZY
BUSY DAY . . .

That **morning** started out just like any other day at the office. I waved hello to my staff, then **scurried** off to my desk. I already knew that there was a **PILE** of work waiting for me — contracts to sign, manuscripts to evaluate, proofs to correct.

Yep, just another crazy busy day.

It's a good thing I love my work, otherwise . . . Oops! I just realized you probably have no idea what I am squeaking about. Let me explain. My name is Stilton, *Geronimo Stilton*. I run *The Rodent's Gazette*, the most famous newspaper on Mouse Island.

Anyway, as I was saying, it's a good thing I **love** my job, otherwise I'd probably want to pull my fur out! From the minute I set paw in the office, the work never stops.

And this Friday was no different. Well, one thing was different. I had decided I would work extra *fast* so I could leave early and get started on my relaxing weekend. The next day was my BIRTHDAY!

But as soon as I sat down, I immediately noticed a *mysterious* envelope on my desk.

It said: For Geronimo Stilton. **PERSONAL**.

CONFIDENTIAL. EXTREMELY URGENT!

I picked it up and stared at it for a long time. *Should I open it?* I wondered.

I don't know why, but for some reason, the envelope filled me with DREAD. My mind raced. My heart pounded. What if it was BAD NEWS? What if someone had died? What if I was being

Should I open it?

sued? What if my **Cheese of the Month Club** subscription had run out?!

Finally, it dawned on me that it might be someone who needed my help. So I opened it. Inside, I found an even more **mysterious** message. . . .

TOMORROW AT NOON, MEET ME AT THE TOP OF MARBLEHEAD MOUNTAIN AT THE POINT MARKED ON THE MAP ON THE BACK OF THIS PAPER.

DON'T BE LATE!

I AM COUNTING ON YOU!

P.S. WHAT TOOK YOU SO LONG TO OPEN THE ENVELOPE, CHEESEBRAIN? I TOLD YOU IT WAS URGENT!

I **GULPED**. Whoever had written those words knew me well. I don't like to **RUSH** things. Yes, even simple things like opening up an envelope. I like to think things through. . . .

And now I had even more to think about. On the back of the paper, there was a map with a path marked out in **RED** leading up to a red **✗**.

I stared at it for a while, then I put it aside. I had a **ton** of work to do. But every time I tried to do something, my mind kept wandering to that **mysterious** message. . . .

Who could have sent it? Who would want to meet on **TOP** of a mountain? After all, almost everyone knows I'm not exactly the most athletic mouse on the block. Just then, I **clapped** my paw to my forehead. Now I knew who sent that message. It had to be my obnoxious cousin **Trap**! He was always playing pranks on me.

I grabbed the **PHONE** and **PUNCHED** in his number.

"Nice try, cousin," I said when he picked up. "You can't fool me. I know you left that **mysterious** message on my desk this morning."

Trap just laughed. "Oooo . . . a **mysterious** message sounds enticing. Wish I had thought of it. But you got the wrong

mouse, Germeister. I've been at the travel agent all morning. I'm planning a little trip to the **Cheesecake Islands**. Have you tried calling Hercule?" he suggested.

That was a good suggestion. My **friend HERCULE POIRAT**, the famous detective, also loved to prank me. But when I called Hercule's cell phone, he insisted the message wasn't from him, either.

"I'm in **TRANSRATANIA** on an investigation, Geronimo," he said. "Some crazy rodent has been dressing up like a refrigerator repair rat and stealing everyone's fridge. It's a nightmare! No one can keep their **cheese** cold, and forget about leftovers!"

Just thinking about cheese made my stomach **growl**. I'd become so worked up about the **mysterious** message I hadn't even had my midmorning snack. How tragic!

I hung up with Hercule and stared at the work in front of me as my stomach rumbled. Then I stared at the message. It was no use. I couldn't concentrate. I had to get to the bottom of this mystery . . . and get some food before I passed out from hunger! Well, okay, maybe I wasn't going to actually faint, but you get the idea.

I grabbed the letter and RUSHED out of the office. My employees ran after me, shouting,

"Geronimo, what about this contract?!"

"Geronimo, what about the MEETING?!"

"Geronimo, what about these Pictures?!"

I dodged past everyone, even my grandfather William, who looked FURIOUS.

"Grandson, how dare you leave this office at this hour!" he bellowed.

But I kept on going.

"Sorry, everyone!" I squeaked. "It's an emergency!"

SORE MUSCLE CREAM?

I was panting by the time I made it outside. Still, there was no time to rest. I had decided the only way to get to the bottom of the mystery was to go to **Marblehead Mountain** the next day. But first I needed to stop at Rat's Authority, the best store in town for sporting goods. If I was going to hike up a mountain, I had to get a new pair of hiking socks. My old ones were filled with moth holes.

The owner of Rat's Authority rubbed his paws together excitedly when he saw me. I tried to tell him that I only wanted **socks**, but he didn't listen.

Instead, he ran around the store picking things up right and left. "You can never be too prepared

when you go **hiking**, Mr. Stilton," he insisted. "You want to make it back **alive**, don't you?"

Before I knew it, I was walking out of the store with a **TON** of bags and boxes. And after all that, I hadn't even bought one pair of socks! I was so **LOADED** up with stuff that I **crashed** into someone coming from the other direction. . . . **Bang!**

All of the packages flew out of my paws, and my head hit the sidewalk with a loud **clunk**! When I stood up, I saw a small mouse with **bright**, warm, caring eyes. It was my dear nephew Benjamin.

"Oh, nephew, I'm so sorry. I got a message, and then the socks, and then I TRIPPED. A-are you okay?" I stammered.

"I'm fine, Uncle," Benjamin answered. "But maybe you should sit down. You're not making

any sense. Here, let me help."

He began stuffing all of my purchases back in the bags.

"Rock climbing ROPE . . . COMPASS, antivenom *serum*, explorer's hat . . . Super Scamper energy bars . . . titanium ice pick . . . radio transmitters . . . anti-blister bandages . . . a maxi-sized tube of cream-cheese-and-chive-scented sore muscle cream . . . SORE muscle cream? Why do you need all of this stuff, Uncle?" Benjamin squeaked, looking confused.

I coughed. I had to admit, I probably didn't need the GIANT tube of sore muscle cream, but how could I resist the cream-cheese-and-chive scent?

I tried to explain to Benjamin about the MYSTERIOUS letter and the meeting at the top of **Marblehead Mountain**. The minute he heard

I was about to go on an adventure, he began jumping up and down.

"Please, Uncle Geronimo, you have to take me with you!" my nephew begged. "I haven't been on an adventure in AGES. Plus, I'm a great climber. You should see me climb the new rock wall at the playground! And, Uncle, you always taught me to never go mountain CLIMBING all by yourself. It's too dangerous."

I smiled. Did I mention my nephew was the smartest mouse ever? Of course, he was right. It would be foolish to climb up a mountain all alone.

"Okay, Benjamin," I agreed. "Let's go plan our trip."

We headed back to my house, and after slurping down one or two cheese smoothies (okay, make that three), we had everything figured out.

14

OF COURSE I CAN CARRY IT!

The next day at DAWN I went to pick up Benjamin. He lives with Aunt Sweetfur, at 2 Ratty Way.

I was wearing an **ENORMOUSE** backpack filled with all of the super-high-tech hiking equipment the mouse at RAT'S AUTHORITY had convinced me I would need to survive.

Unfortunately, he didn't mention I would need

Argh!

ENORMOUSE muscles in order to carry everything. My pack weighed a **ton**! I could barely take a step without stopping to catch my breath. Forget climbing **Marblehead Mountain**, I'd be lucky if I survived the trip to Aunt Sweetfur's!

When I finally arrived, Benjamin was waiting for me with his own compact backpack. His eyes grew **HUGE** when he saw all of the stuff I was carrying.

"Um, Uncle, do you think you are going to be able to carry that pack **ALL THE WAY** up the mountain? It looks pretty **heavy**," he squeaked.

What could I do? I didn't want Benjamin to think his uncle was a weakling. So I forced a smile and said, "This little old thing? Of course I can carry it."

With that, we headed to the train station and boarded the first train to **Marblehead Mountain**.

Two hours later, we arrived at our destination

and began trekking up the very **STEEP** path that led to the top of the mountain. As we climbed, **deadly** ravines opened up at every turn, rocks **crumbled** beneath our paws, and what were those scary **howling** noises? Wolves?

Now I knew why they called this place **Marblehead Mountain**. You'd have to have a head full of **marbles** to climb it!

Even though I was **shaking** with fear and exhaustion, I did my best to lead the way. I didn't want Benjamin to worry.

Finally, after about five hundred hours (well, okay, maybe it was only twenty minutes), I suggested we take a break. I plopped down on the ground and pulled out my box of **Super Scamper** energy bars. Benjamin ate a little piece, but I **GOBBLED** down an entire bar in one gulp. Then, just to help

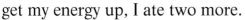

get my energy up, I ate two more.

Benjamin tried to stop me. "Careful, Uncle! It says one bar fills you up for an entire week!" he **squeaked**, reading aloud from the wrapper.

But it was too late. I began to feel my mouth get **THICK** and my stomach get heavy.

It was then that I realized I hadn't brought a **WATER** bottle and Benjamin hadn't filled his **WATER** bottle up.

So I told my nephew I'd be back, and ventured off the trail toward a stream I spotted in the distance. But within seconds, I **slipped** on a rock and began to tumble down . . . down . . . down . . . down . . . down . . .

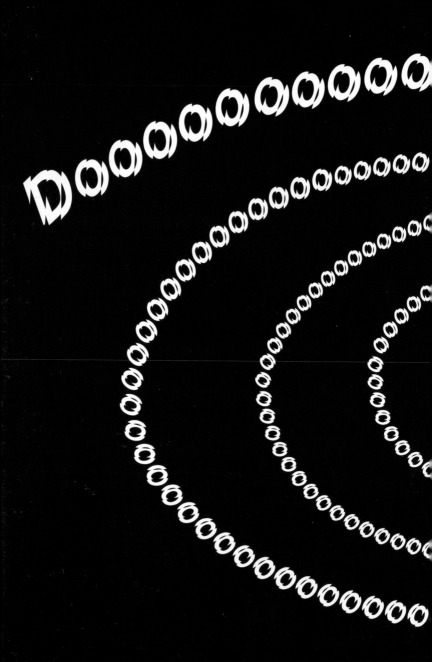

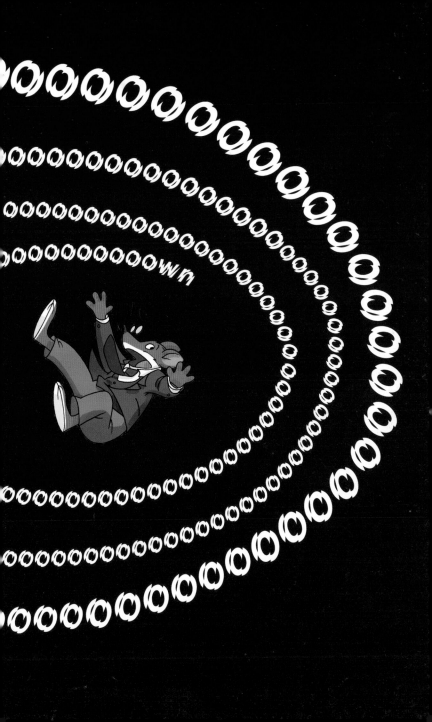

I landed at the bottom of a **mysterious** cave. I'd like to tell you more about what it was like, but a minute later I fainted.

I have no idea how long I was out, but when I **slowly** opened my eyes, I found myself in a very strange place. It was lit by a mysterious **green** light.

was I DREaMiNG?

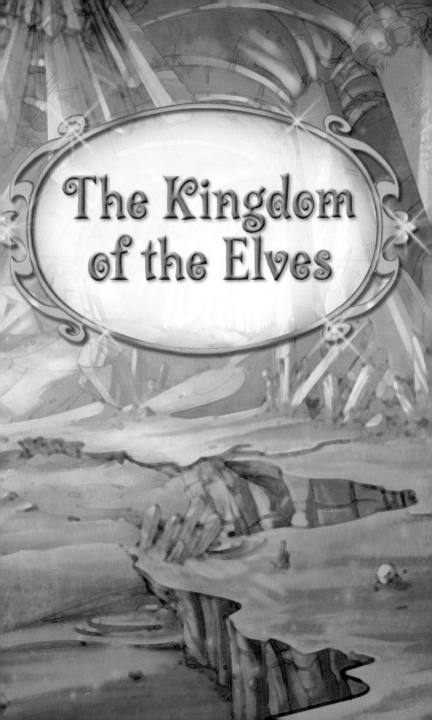

The Kingdom
of the Elves

Welcome to the Kingdom of the Elves!

This is the Cave of the Ancient Kings, or rather the secret entrance to the Kingdom of the Elves. It is a deep and vast emerald cave through which only those with a pure heart can pass. Evil creatures will be blocked in the cave by emerald giants who emerge from crystals in the ground.

1. The Street of the Lost Traveler
2. The Pathway of Marvels
3. The Crossroads of This Way or That Way
4. The Passage of the Morning Light
5. Emerald Guardians
6. The Secret Tunnel (leads to the Room of the Ancient Kings)
7. Sincerity Lake
8. Whispering Pillars
9. The Great Emerald Stalactite

WELCOME TO THE KINGDOM OF THE ELVES, KNIGHT!

I took off my glasses and cleaned them. Then I put them back on. I blinked. Yep, the green light was still there. And as I looked around, I soon realized that the startling green light was coming from the walls of an incredible cave made entirely of sparkling emeralds! Even more startling, I was not alone!

In front of me was an elegant MAIDEN dressed in green. She had long, curly hair the color of emeralds. On her forehead she wore a small golden crown with the symbol of an oak leaf, the emblem of the elves of the forest.

Behind her stood three young elf warriors. They had bows and arrows on their backs.

"Welcome to the Kingdom of the Elves, Knight!" the maiden said with a warm smile.

I blinked again. "Um, w-w-where d-d-did you say I am, miss?" I stammered.

The green maiden laughed. "You are in the Kingdom of Fantasy. Well, to be more precise, you are in the **CAVE OF THE ANCIENT KINGS**, the secret entrance to the Kingdom of the Elves. I am Princess **Emerald**, but everyone calls me Em. My brother, King Thunderhorn, sent me."

Now I was totally confused. How did I get to the **KINGDOM**

Welcome, Knight!

OF FANTASY? I usually arrived on the back of the Dragon of the Rainbow. He'd show up at my bedroom window at night and whisk me away.

Oh well, at least I knew who **KING THUNDERHORN** was. He used to be a deer. Well, first he was an **ELF**, then he was turned into a DEER, then he became an **ELF** again. Talk about confusing! Still, Thunderhorn never told me he had a sister.

"I'm not surprised," Em **snorted** when I told her. "My brother always forgets me. But it doesn't matter. The important thing is that you are here. We need your help!"

Her face grew very serious as she continued. "The situation is out of control, Sir Geronimo. **TERRIBLE** things are happening in our kingdom and in all of the **KINGDOM OF FANTASY**. That is why my brother sent for you. Don't worry — he will explain everything to you. But now we'd better go."

I hobbled after the princess. I must have had a

EMERALD AND THUNDERHORN

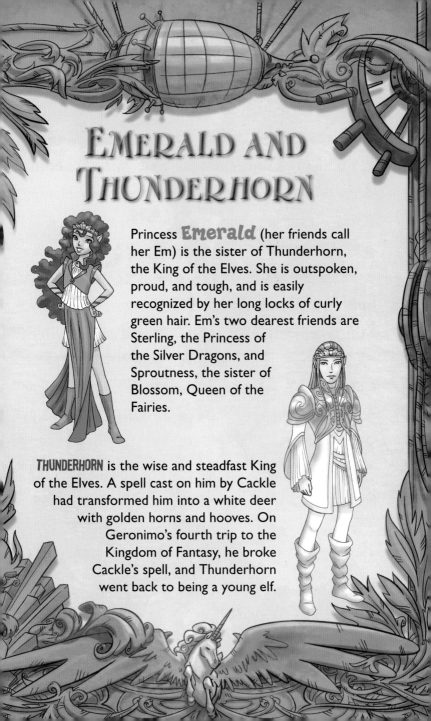

Princess **Emerald** (her friends call her Em) is the sister of Thunderhorn, the King of the Elves. She is outspoken, proud, and tough, and is easily recognized by her long locks of curly green hair. Em's two dearest friends are Sterling, the Princess of the Silver Dragons, and Sproutness, the sister of Blossom, Queen of the Fairies.

THUNDERHORN is the wise and steadfast King of the Elves. A spell cast on him by Cackle had transformed him into a white deer with golden horns and hooves. On Geronimo's fourth trip to the Kingdom of Fantasy, he broke Cackle's spell, and Thunderhorn went back to being a young elf.

bad fall. Even my tail was sore!

Suddenly, Em stopped and stared at me. "No offense, Knight, but you need to change. That outfit won't protect you from all of the **DANGERS** around here," she said.

DANGERS? My teeth chattered. Then one of the elves handed me my armor.

Immediately, I felt a little better. There's nothing like a suit of armor to give a mouse **courage**!

Unbreakable boots

Flexible tail cover

Hard head helmet

Brave belt

Punch-proof chest prote

As soon as I was ready, we headed inside the **CAVE OF THE ANCIENT KINGS**. I pointed to tiny emeralds poking out from the floor around us, right next to the pathway.

Em grinned. "Those are the **EMERALD GUARDIANS**. They only let those with a pure heart pass, Knight. If you are **evil**, they block your path and turn as **tall** as towers," she explained.

Holey cheese! And I thought they were just pretty stones!

For you, Knight!

Thank you!

The princess led the way down corridors carved from **emerald**, past rooms decorated with columns, and up **STEEP** steps that were as **SLIPPERY** as glass.

Finally, we reached a circular room. We were surrounded by eight incredibly **TALL** emerald statues, each wearing a **GOLD** crown.

"These are the statues of the ancient kings and queens that reigned over our kingdom from the beginning and beyond," the princess said. The statues looked so real, it was a little **creepy**. I almost felt as if one of them might start **talking** at any moment!

Beyond the statues was a **STONE** door.

The princess told me to open it, so I did. Flying furballs!

THE KINGDOM OF THE ELVES WAS BREATHTAKING!

THE SECRET DOOR TO THE KINGDOM OF THE ELVES

I took a step and the heavy **STONE** door slammed behind me with a really loud **bang**. Squeak! Watch the tail!

BANG!

Squeak!

"This is one of the secret entrances to the KINGDOM OF THE ELVES," said the princess, her tone turning serious. "Reveal it to no one."

A far-off echo repeated her last words:

TO NO ONE ...   TO NO ONE ...
TO NO ONE ...
O NO ONE ...   TO NO ONE ...   TO NO ONE ...

"Don't worry, Princess Em, your SECRET is safe with me," I assured her. And I meant it. I am the **best** at keeping SECRETS. Well, except for that one time when I gave away Trap's hiding place in a game of *hide-and-seek*. What could I do? He was hiding in the **clothes dryer**. It just wasn't safe!

For a moment, we stood at the entrance to the Kingdom, admiring the view. The princess proudly pointed out to me all of the incredible MOUNTAINS, lakes, waterfalls, and rivers.

It was so **beautiful** I felt like I was dreaming. . . .

Too bad the feeling didn't last long. Right then, one of the elves came **running** over to us.

"Princess Em, we must **hurry**. The road ahead is long, and recently there have been many earthqua —"

Before he could finish his sentence, the ground began to shake. Rocks **CRASHED** down all around us.

"Help! Earthquake!"

I yelled in full-on panic mode. Oh, how I hate natural disasters!

Suddenly, the earth **cracked** open and I began to fall. "Good-bye, world!" I sobbed hysterically. But at the last second, my tail caught on a piece of rock, and I was left **dangling** over the edge.

After about two hundred HOURS (okay, it was only two minutes, but it felt like forever!), the earth stopped **shaking**, and the elves pulled me to safety.

I was a little embarrassed for crying like a mouseling, but what could I say?

I was **scared out of my fur**!

As soon as I pulled myself together, we headed down the **steep** path that led to the valley and **Deer Castle**. The princess explained that **THUNDERHORN** would be waiting for us at the castle.

The damaging effects of the **earthquake** were all around us. Everywhere we looked we saw **fallen** trees, **wrecked** shrubs, and **plunging** rifts in the earth like the one that had almost swallowed me. Floods had covered forests and fields, and the clear lakes that just recently had **sparkled** in the sun were now reduced to muddy pools.

It was a completely changed landscape. What a **terrible** tragedy. How could the kingdom recover from such a **MESS**?

Tears ROLLED down Em's cheeks as she surveyed the damage. Even the ancient elfin forest, the heart of the KINGDOM OF THE ELVES, was being **threatened** by dark cracks where the earth had split open all around us.

"I've been in earthquakes before, but this was the worst one yet," the princess **wailed**. "In fact, the earthquakes are one of the reasons why my brother sent for you. But honestly, Knight, I don't see how you can help."

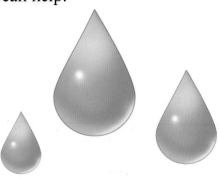

I NEED YOUR HELP!

I didn't want to upset the princess, so I kept silent. But she was right. I couldn't stop an earthquake. Thunderhorn needed a **SUPERHERO**, not a **SCAREDY-MOUSE**!

Soon, we reached **Deer Castle** and entered the greeting room. It was decorated with scenes from elfin history. There was even one with me in it.

It was a picture from my fourth voyage to the **KINGDOM OF FANTASY**, when Thunderhorn and I had saved each other's lives. Under the painting,

FRIENDS FOREVER

there were two words:

FRIENDS FOREVER

I smiled, remembering. Just then, a voice broke my thoughts. "Hello, Knight! I'm so glad you came!"

It was my friend Thunderhorn!

It was good to see him. Although I must admit, I was still getting used to seeing him as a prince and not a white deer.

We shook hooves . . . I mean hands . . . I mean paws. Er, well, you know what I mean. Then **THUNDERHORN** said, "Knight, I need your help. Let me show you what has happened to my kingdom."

We **CLIMBED** to the top of one of the castle turrets.

All over the Kingdom, elves were busy repairing everything that had been destroyed during the earthquakes. Some were filling in large **cracks** in the land. Some were replanting trees. Some were **STACKING**

DEER CASTLE

This ancient castle was built at the time of Silvan I the Wise, the first king of the Oak dynasty, the king of all the elves. Since then, all the kings and queens of the elves live here. It is a solid and welcoming structure, but it is also an impenetrable castle, because the access to the valley it sits in is top secret, and its walls are built with stones from the Valley of Giants.

In case of attack, the Silver Woods will transform into an impenetrable barrier of silver branches and leaves, which will protect the castle and its inhabitants.

1. KING THUNDERHORN'S QUARTERS
2. GREAT TOWER OF THE ELVES OF GREENWOOD FOREST
3. GUARDS' QUARTERS AND BOW STORAGE
4. EMERALD'S QUARTERS
5. PROTECT AND ADMIRE TOWER
6. TOWER OF THE HAPPY ELF
7. SPARKLING RIVER
8. SWEETWATER MOAT
9. SILVER WOODS

bags of sand along the riverbank to prevent **flooding**.

"The **earthquakes** started just a week ago," Thunderhorn murmured sadly. "There is so much damage. And though we are repairing everything, I'm **AFRAID** the earthquakes will keep happening.

"That is why I sent for you, **KNIGHT**," Thunderhorn continued. "I need to figure out why we keep having these **earthquakes**. Will you help?" he asked.

I didn't want to burst Thunderhorn's bubble, but what could a mouse like me do? I was a publisher, not a scientist. I knew a lot about books, but I didn't know anything about the *shifting* earth and weather **PatteRns**. Still, the elf prince looked so depressed, I nodded my head yes.

"I knew I could count on you!" Thunderhorn grinned.

KNOWITALLOLOGISTS?

We headed down the **STONE STEPS** that led back to the greeting room. As we walked, I prayed that a brilliant idea for how to help would hit me, but the only thing I got hit with was a **FALLING** tree branch. YOUCH!

By the time we reached the greeting room, I decided it would be best if I just was honest with Thunderhorn. "I think you need a scientist to help you," I told my friend. "The only thing I know about is *books*."

To my surprise, Thunderhorn's grin broadened. "Exactly, Knight!" he said excitedly. "I need a **BOOK-SMART** mouse like you to travel to a place called the *Great Explanatorium*. It's where all of the brilliant scientists of the **KINGDOM OF FANTASY** live: volcanologists, geologists, meteorologists, witchologists, ogreologists, trollologists, knowitallologists . . ."

KNOWITALLOLOGISTS? I was beginning to think maybe the prince had been hit in the head with a tree branch himself, when Princess Em arrived.

"Did my brother tell you about the *Great Explanatorium*?" she asked with a strange smile.

Thunderhorn ignored her. "Anyway, Knight," he continued. "You can ask the experts about the earthquakes. Of course, I'd go myself, but I've got this terrible **blister** on my toe, and . . ."

At this, the princess **burst** out laughing.

Ha, ha, ha!

Humph!

"Come on, brother," she giggled. "Tell the knight the **truth**. You don't want to go there because you don't want to see your old teacher, `Professor Longwind`."

Thunderhorn **blushed**. "Okay, okay," he agreed. "My sister is right. I was a terrible student in school. I preferred practicing with swords and bows and arrows over studying. And I liked to play pranks on poor `Professor Longwind`."

It was hard to picture the prince as a **disobedient** elf. He seemed so responsible

Oops . . .

How dare you?

now. But I guess it is true what they say — we all grow up sooner or later. Then again, that didn't really explain my cousin Trap. He's been playing pranks on me since we were mouselings in **HIGH CHAIRS**!

"The worst part is, **Professor Longwind** is now the chancellor of the *Great Explanatorium*. I would like to tell him I am sorry for being such a **TROUBLEMAKER**. But I'm afraid he may still be **MAD** at me and refuse to help my kingdom," Thunderhorn lamented.

I told the prince not to worry. I would take the trip to the Great Explanatorium. After all, what are friends for? I didn't mention that I was scared out of my fur to make the journey. Thunderhorn had described the trek as **LONG** and **dangerous**. Rats!

Lucky for me, Princess Em insisted she

THREE INSEPARABLE FRIENDS!

Princesses Sterling, Emerald, and Sproutness are great friends.

Sterling is the Princess of the Silver Dragons. She is a skilled dragon tamer who trains dragons using her silver flute. Her favorite dragon is named Sparkle. She is an expert swordswoman and an archer with amazing aim.

Emerald (known to her friends as Em) is the Princess of the Elves and the sister of King Thunderhorn. She has long curly hair that is a rich emerald color. She is tough and brave and never afraid to speak her mind.

Sproutness is the Princess of the Fairies and sister to Queen Blossom. She is the Fairy of the Earth and can make seedlings sprout from the ground just by singing! She also has the power to grant seven wishes using an enchanted medallion she received from Blossom, her sister.

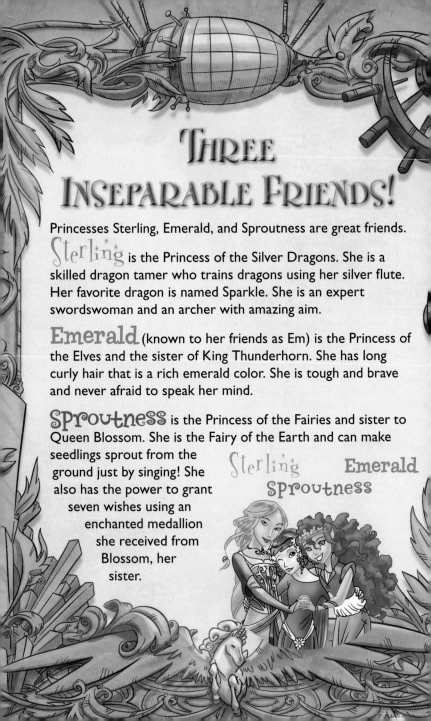

Sterling Emerald
Sproutness

accompany me. "I can visit with my friends Sterling and Sproutness," she said happily.

"Okay, you two, but be CAREFUL," Thunderhorn warned. "Many have gone to the Great Explanatorium with questions, but few have returned. The answers are there, but you often must wait a LONG, LONG, LONG time to get them. It could be days, weeks, months, years. . . ."

Holey cheese! I pictured my fur GRAYING as I waited for an answer from this crazy place. My heart began beating a mile a minute. What a NIGHTMARE!

Thunderhorn interrupted my thoughts. "But we need an answer very soon, to STOP this destruction!"

Here is the symbol of the Kingdom of the Elves.

An elf arrived carrying a map that was sealed with the symbol of the KINGDOM OF THE ELVES: two oak leaves and an acorn.

"This is a map of the KINGDOM OF FANTASY," Thunderhorn said. "As long as you hold it, you will never get LOST. In five days, I will meet you outside the *Great Explanatorium*. Good luck, Knight. I am counting on you."

"I'll get your answer," I told the king as we set out the next day. "Don't **worry**."

Now if only *I* could stop *worrying*!

Be careful!

See you soon!

Good-bye!

The Great
Explanatorium

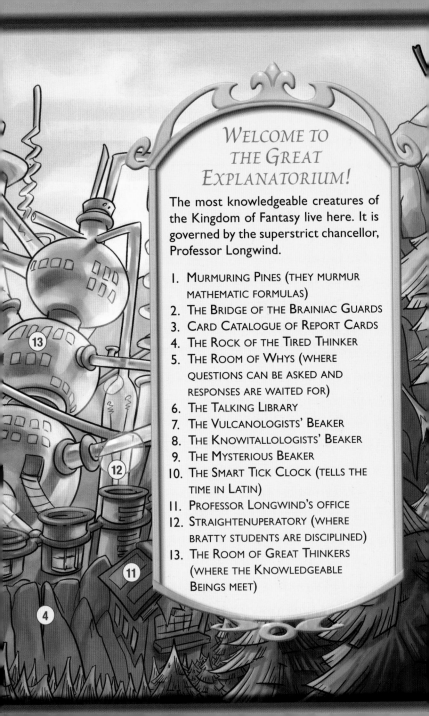

WELCOME TO THE GREAT EXPLANATORIUM!

The most knowledgeable creatures of the Kingdom of Fantasy live here. It is governed by the superstrict chancellor, Professor Longwind.

1. MURMURING PINES (THEY MURMUR MATHEMATIC FORMULAS)
2. THE BRIDGE OF THE BRAINIAC GUARDS
3. CARD CATALOGUE OF REPORT CARDS
4. THE ROCK OF THE TIRED THINKER
5. THE ROOM OF WHYS (WHERE QUESTIONS CAN BE ASKED AND RESPONSES ARE WAITED FOR)
6. THE TALKING LIBRARY
7. THE VULCANOLOGISTS' BEAKER
8. THE KNOWITALLOLOGISTS' BEAKER
9. THE MYSTERIOUS BEAKER
10. THE SMART TICK CLOCK (TELLS THE TIME IN LATIN)
11. PROFESSOR LONGWIND'S OFFICE
12. STRAIGHTENUPERATORY (WHERE BRATTY STUDENTS ARE DISCIPLINED)
13. THE ROOM OF GREAT THINKERS (WHERE THE KNOWLEDGEABLE BEINGS MEET)

DON'T SAY IT!

The trip to the Great Explanatorium was hard and dangerous. We encountered **earthquake** tremors, landslides, and rifts along our path.

Finally, we reached the top of a steep hill. Spread out before us we could see the *Great Explanatorium*.

The city was so **strange**! The buildings seemed to be made entirely out of **glass**, and were shaped like the kinds of beakers you use in a science experiment, connected by long **coils**.

I **twisted** my tail *nervously*. What was this place?

Suddenly, a **cold** hand gripped my shoulder. "Please, d-d-don't **HURT** me!" I cried.

But it was only Princess Em. She told me she was going to continue on to the **KINGDOM OF**

the silver dragons to see her friends.

We waved good-bye. I approached the entrance of the *Great Explanatorium* on shaky paws. There, I was examined by two guards dressed in robes and wearing hats shaped like upside-down books.

"I am Stilton . . . I mean, er, Sir Geronimo of Stilton," I said. "I am here on an URGENT MISSION. I must speak to Chancellor **Professor Longwind** right away. King **THUNDERHORN** sent me."

Interesting . . .

Very unusual . . .

As soon as I said the name **THUNDERHORN**, the two guards froze.

"What did you say?" one asked.

"King **THUNDERHORN** sent me," I repeated.

"Who?" the second guard asked.

At this point, I was starting to think they had hearing problems, so I **YELLED**:

"KING THUNDERHORN SENT ME!"

This sent the two guards into a **panic**.

One raised a finger to his lips. "**Shhhhh!**" he hissed. "You **cannot** — correction — you **must not** speak that name!"

The other was **RUNNING IN CIRCLES** with his hands over his ears.

How **bizarre**! I wondered what would

happen if I said the name **THUNDERHORN** again. But I didn't have time to find out. **THUNDERHORN** was counting on me! So I told the guards about my urgent question.

The first guard said, "It's simple. First you place a request at counter **132**, get the form from window **321**, deliver it to window **231**, make sure it's not **213**, then return to window **132**, and they will give you the answer. **Got it**?"

Got it?

Um, well, actually . . .

?!

RATS! I hadn't understood a thing!

The guard led me to a room filled with **really long** lines of people waiting in front of windows.

They all looked *exhausted*. Some had fallen asleep and were **snoring**.

Gulp! "Um, how **LONG** do you think it will take to get an answer?" I asked worriedly.

"Depends on the question," he said. "It could take a month . . . a year . . . a CENTURY . . ."

"But I can't wait!" I shrieked. "I need an answer

immediately. The **ELFIN FOREST** is in danger! It's a matter of **life and death**!"

The guard scratched his chin SLOWLY. "Well, I guess, for urgent cases like yours, they might make an exception and let you ask your QUESTION directly to the chancellor during the next Great Council."

I can't wait!

"Great!" I squeaked. "Let's go!"

"Hold on," the GUARD replied. "First, I must see if you are allowed

in the ROOM OF GREAT THINKERS. Only the most dedicated students may enter."

He brought me to a room lined with ROWS of filing cabinets, which apparently held all the report cards of all the students in the world! Then he opened a folder labeled "Sir Geronimo of Stilton," and started to dig through my school file.

Lucky for me, I had been a pretty good student. When the guard saw my report cards, he nodded and put a **stamp** on a scroll.

It read:

This certifies that the Knight is a serious student and may enter the Room of Great Thinkers.

Signed,
The First Guard

The guard checked his watch and **yawned**. "Better hurry. The next meeting is in exactly . . . **one minute and twelve seconds**. Oh, and if you're late, you're out of luck."

Cheese sticks!

I ran as fast as my paws could carry me!

Cheese sticks!

BLAH BLAH BLAH . . .

I made it to the ROOM OF GREAT THINKERS and burst inside. The circular room was lined with tall bleachers where many **wise** and **SERIOUS** thinkers from all over the **KINGDOM OF FANTASY** had gathered. There were scientists, mathematicians, volcanologists, geologists, witchologists, ogreologists, trollologists, and even **KNOWITALLOLOGISTS**! It was just like **THUNDERHORN** had said!

I was so busy looking around, I didn't notice an owl with **ENORMOUSE** glasses approaching me. "Who? Who? Who are you?" he demanded.

The crowd turned to stare at me with suspicious eyes. My fur turned **RED** with embarrassment.

"Um, I am *Sir Stilton of Geronimo* — I mean *Sir Geronimo of Stilton*, and I have a magnificent question — I mean a question for Professor Magnificent — I mean a Professor **Longwind** question . . ." I babbled.

Oh, why do I turn into such a **BLITHERING** fool when I get nervous?

Finally, I took a deep breath and shouted, "I have a question for the magnificent **Professor Longwind!**"

At that moment, a man's **THIN** face poked out from behind a **LARGE** desk that was piled

Who? Who? Who are you?

I am Sir Stilton of Geronimo....

high with books. He was wearing a long **DARK** robe and the same open-book hat that the guards had on their heads. The only difference was his hat was made out of **GOLD**. He leaned toward me and said in a bored voice, "**QUESTIONS, QUESTIONS,** always more **QUESTIONS.**"

Just then the **WISE** owl flew over to the desk and began complaining to the professor.

"You know, Chancellor, it's getting late," he said. "Maybe we should call it a night. There's always tomorrow, and the next day, and the next **month**, and the next **year**. . . ."

But the professor just brushed him aside. He picked up a wooden **mallet** and hit it hard against the desk.

Bang!

"Continue with your question, Sir Knight!" he demanded.

So I told him about the **earthquakes** that were destroying the **KINGDOM OF FANTASY**. "Why are they happening?" I asked.

Immediately, all of the experts in the room began to *talk* at the same time. Then they began to **argue** with each other. Then **shout**.

I felt a giant headache coming on.

Finally, Professor Longwind picked up his mallet and slammed it down.

"*SILEEEENCE!*" he shrieked.

When the room settled down, he cleared his throat and said, "Friends, esteemed colleagues, and our visitor from afar, I will be *brief*."

Unfortunately, the Professor's idea of *brief* was more like never-ending!

"The knight needs to know the cause of these earthquakes, and since he's in a rush, we will follow the URGENT procedures for URGENT answers to URGENT

I think . . .

I, on the other hand, believe . . .

No, I believe . . .

Whaaat?!

questions. Everyone will get a chance to speak, but be brief and wait your turn! I will start. Now, as you know, the **KINGDOM OF FANTASY** has never had **earthquakes** until now, but according to the Sudden Shake theory, there may be tremors because something has *frightened* the land! Or, according to the **HiccuPiSmS** theory, the Kingdom may have quakes because it has the *hiccups*! Or, if you follow the **CHUCKLES** theory, it's because when we plow the fields we are *tickling* them!"

He continued to explain ridiculous theories, until I fell ASLEEP as he was blabbing on. "*Blah blah blah . . . blah blah blah blah . . . blah blah blah . . . blah blah blah . . . blah blah blah . . .*"

EARTHQUAKES
In the real world, earthquakes occur when two plates that form the earth's crust (similar to very large blocks of land) suddenly slip past each other, releasing energy and shaking the ground above.

DID SOMEONE SAY "THUNDERHORN"?

When I woke up, I realized that it was **dawn**. Professor Longwind had talked all night long! I don't know if I've ever met anyone so **long-winded**!

At that point I decided I had to interrupt. Time was **RUNNING** out! So I said politely, "Excuse me, Professor, but could you maybe summarize, or, um, **wrap** things up? I need an urgent answer for my friend **THUNDERHORN**."

As soon as I said the word **THUNDERHORN**, I covered my mouth, but it was **too late**!

The room fell **SILENT**....

Professor Longwind stopped talking instantly. His eyes grew

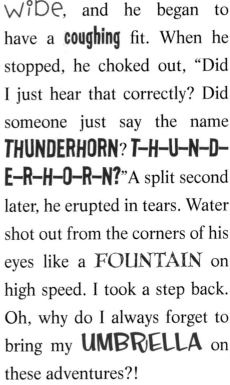

Did someone say "Thunderhorn"?

The one and only Thunderhorn?

Thunderhorn Thunderhorn Thunderhorn?

WIDE, and he began to have a **coughing** fit. When he stopped, he choked out, "Did I just hear that correctly? Did someone just say the name **THUNDERHORN**? **T–H–U–N–D–E–R–H–O–R–N?**" A split second later, he erupted in tears. Water shot out from the corners of his eyes like a FOUNTAIN on high speed. I took a step back. Oh, why do I always forget to bring my **UMBRELLA** on these adventures?!

"**THUNDERHORN**, the only student I was never able to teach my massive amounts of knowledge to," he wailed to no one in particular. "He said my lessons were **boring**. He said he'd rather train with his sword. He said he'd rather **climb** trees. . . ."

The owl **GLARED** at me. "Now look what you've done. He's going to cry for hours. Didn't anyone warn you not to mention the name **THUNDERHORN**?" he griped.

Unfortunately, the professor was within earshot and began to cry even harder. Puddles formed at his feet. I had to think of something fast before we all **DROWNED**!

"It's okay, Professor," I said, handing him my handkerchief. "My friend the *King of the Elves* told me that he is **sorry**, and he even wanted to **thank you** for all the things you taught him."

At this the professor suddenly stopped crying.

GRATITUDE

Gratitude is a very important virtue. It means being thankful to someone who has done something nice for us and expressing our thanks in a kind way.

"**REALLY?**" he said. "How nice! And now I will give a short lecture on gratitude. So . . . *blah blah blah . . .*"

Before I could stop him, he had launched into another long, long, long lecture.

I **GROANED** inwardly. At this rate, I'd never get my earthquake answer from the professor! A few minutes later, a grasshopper in a smart coat **HOPPED** over to me.

"Knight, if you're in a rush to find an answer, I would suggest you try checking out the **Talking Library**. You can find a ton of answers there. Just be careful," he advised.

I was going to ask him why they called it the **Talking Library** and why I had to be careful, but before I could, he hopped away.

When I reached the library, I sighed happily. The room was filled with a familiar SCENT. . . .

READ ME!

Mmmm . . . I just love the scent of **BOOKS**!

I entered the library and immediately noticed a **lectern** with a book on it and some strange instructions.

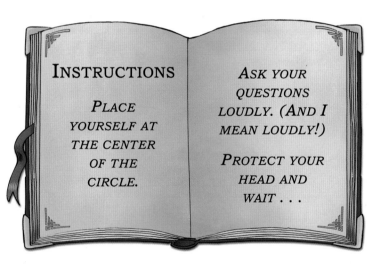

INSTRUCTIONS

PLACE YOURSELF AT THE CENTER OF THE CIRCLE.

ASK YOUR QUESTIONS LOUDLY. (AND I MEAN LOUDLY!)

PROTECT YOUR HEAD AND WAIT . . .

I had nothing to lose, so I did exactly what the **instructions** said. First, I moved the lectern aside

and stood in the center of the circle on the floor. Then I asked in a **trembling** voice, "What is the cause of the earthquakes that are destroying the **KINGDOM OF FANTASY**?"

When I was done asking my question, a **MYSTERIOUS** voice called out, "Can't you **READ**?! It says to ask your question **LOUDLY**!"

So I did. Then I *shut* my eyes, **DUCKED** my head, and waited. . . .

What is the cause . . .

Ask your question loudly . . .

Protect your head and wait .

Suddenly, a spot on the floor quivered, and the bookshelves filled with books began to shake. Then books of all shapes and sizes began to fling themselves at me. As they flew through the air, they SCREAMED:

"Read me!"

"No, me!"

"Hey, watch the **spine**!"

"I was here first!"

. . . and the books with your answer will arrive from the air!

In a flash, I was completely buried under a **mountain** of books!

I should have known. What else would be in a TALKING Library but talking books!

As soon as I **CLIMBED** out of the pile, I held up my paw for SILENCE. "Please, everyone, be quiet. We are in a library, after all," I squeaked.

SHHHHHHHHHHH!

Then I asked the books to **DIVIDE** themselves
into subjects. "On the right, I want books about
earthquakes, and on the left, I want books about
volcanoes. . . ." I began.

Pushing and **shoving**, the books tried
to organize themselves, but every few minutes
another fight would break out. They all wanted
to be on the top of the pile so I would read them
first. They screamed and shouted:

"Read me first! I've got **COLOR** pictures!"

"Big deal, I've got a pull-out **MAP**!"

"Oh, yeah? Well, I've got a genuine **LeatHer**
binding!"

After a while, they were **SCREAMING** so
loud, I could barely hear myself squeak. I couldn't
believe it. I love books — but these books were
driving me **CRAZY**!

At last, I managed to get them to **ORGANIZE**
themselves alphabetically. "I will read all of you,

rodent's honor!" I promised.

And I did. It took me a full day and full night to read them all. I learned many things about **earthquakes** and **volcanoes**. Too bad I didn't find the **answer** to my question.

EARTHQUAKE: the shaking, rolling, or sudden shock of the earth's surface.

VOLCANO: a mountain in the shape of a cone, with a crater that may expel lava, ash, and smoke.

EPICENTER: the point on the earth's surface that is directly above the focus of an earthquake; the point where it begins.

TREMORS: trembling or shaking after an earthquake has taken place.

None of the books explained why the ground had been **shaking** for a week. They also didn't say why there had never been **earthquakes** in the Kingdom of Fantasy before.

I did discover one interesting thing, though. It seemed that all earthquakes are STRONGEST at a point that is called the epicenter. I decided there was only one thing to do. I'd have to go to the epicenter to see what was going on. I pulled the map of the KINGDOM OF FANTASY out of my bag and marked a red spot at the point where I thought the epicenter was: the Volcano of Fire!

My whiskers trembled with fright.

The books were sad to see me leave. They ruffled their pages and waved bookmarks as I headed out the door.

"Come back and see us again, Knight!" called a large encyclopedia.

"Hope you got a lot of info from me!" piped up a small **red** pocket dictionary.

"Uh, no offense, **Red**, but you pocket editions are a little short on content," insisted a leather-bound reference book with faded GOLD letters.

"Oh, and you think you're better with those old pages? When was the last time you were updated?" shot back the dictionary.

I could tell the books were about to start **fighting** again, so I quickly slipped out the door. **Whew!** I never thought I'd be so **HAPPY** to get away from a stack of books!

UNITED FOREVER

I left the Great Explanatorium feeling like a zombie mouse. I was sooooo tired. It felt like I had been AWAKE for a month reading that mountain of books. It was actually only **one** day and night, but still . . . I was pooped! I sat down under a big tree to wait for my friends. But within seconds I was out like a light.

Snore! Snore! Snore!

When I woke up, I let out a **LOUD**, satisfying yawn, stretched, and scratched under my armpit. CHEESE NIBLETS, I felt refreshed! I was just beginning to scratch my tail (that armor sure is itchy!) when I realized I wasn't alone. Thunderhorn, Princess Em, and Sterling, the Princess of the Silver Dragons, stood staring down at me with serious expressions. How **EMBARRASSING**!

"Uh, what's going on?" I asked.

"Terrible news, Knight!" Em cried. "Our friend Sproutness is missing!"

"She was supposed to come to my kingdom a week ago, but she never arrived," Sterling explained. "I sent my **DRAGONS** out to find her, but they could only find this **MEDALLION**. It's a gift from **Blossom**, her sister. She would never part with it."

"This is awful!" sobbed Em. "Maybe **Sproutness** has been kidnapped!"

Sterling showed me the medallion. In the center were the letters **S** and **B**, Sproutness and Blossom's initials. Around them were seven **STONES**, each a different color of the **rainbow**. On the back was an inscription in the **Fantasian alphabet**. It said:

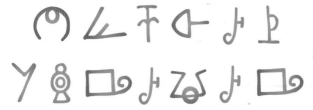

Can you translate it?*

SPROUTNESS'S MEDALLION

This medallion was a gift from Blossom, the Queen of the Fairies, to Sproutness, her sister. It is a symbol of the love that unites them. On the back, there is an inscription that reads: "United forever." It is a charmed medallion. It can fulfill seven wishes, one for each stone.

Right then, I felt a pang of homesickness. I thought of my family. My adventurous sister, Thea, my sweet nephew Benjamin, and my annoying cousin Trap. Oh, how I missed them!

> **LOVE AND DISTANCE**
> Great distances are not enough to erase strong feelings, because the family and true friends we love stay in our hearts forever.

I was still thinking about my family when Em said, "I just remembered — Sproutness told me that this medallion is enchanted! It can grant **seven** wishes."

I wasn't sure about the whole **ENCHANTED** thing. I mean, how could a medallion **GRANT** wishes? Still, I closed my eyes, clasped the medallion, and wished it could lead us to Sproutness.

But when I opened my eyes, nothing happened. Everyone stared at me. So I tried again. And again. And again. Nothing happened.

Finally, totally **frustrated**, I closed my

eyes and shrieked,

"WHERE IS SPROUTNESS?!"

This time when I opened my eyes, the medallion was releasing a **RED** ray of light in the shape of an **ARROW**. It was pointing due west!

"That's where I was headed!" I cried. "It's leading us to the Volcano of Fire!"

When the arrow DISAPPEARED, I noticed that one of the stones had turned from **RED** to gray and didn't sparkle anymore. The medallion had granted its first wish, and there were only six left. I promised myself I would not waste them. It wouldn't be easy. We were headed for a **DANGEROUS** volcano. It would take all of my **willpower** not to wish I was back in my **cozy** home!

GOOD-BYE, PRINCESS EM!

We headed immediately in the direction the **RED** ➤ arrow had pointed.

Princess Emerald led the way, her **GREEN** hair **waving** like a flag behind her. But after a few minutes, **THUNDERHORN** called for her to stop.

"Em, I know you want to be the one to find your friend, but I need you to go back to **Deer Castle**. The elves are without a leader, and I need you to watch over our kingdom while I'm away," he said.

At first, the princess put up a **FUSS**, but when Thunderhorn refused to change his mind, she gave up.

"Okay, okay," she agreed. "I'll go back. But I hope you know I'm not **happy** about this,

Deer
Castle

brother!" she insisted, **STOMPING** her feet.

After the princess had calmed down, she **HUGGED** Sterling good-bye. Then she **HUGGED** me. And finally, she **HUGGED** Thunderhorn.

"Don't worry, sis. I promise we will find Sproutness and bring her home," he assured her.

"You'd better," Em called back as she headed down the road.

"**SISTERS**," Thunderhorn muttered.

Once Princess Em had disappeared from sight, we continued westward toward the **Volcano of Fire**. It was tough going. As we walked, the **tremors** became stronger and stronger, and rocks **tumbled** down around us. It was clear that we were really reaching the epicenter — the place where the **earthquakes** were coming from. I tried not to think about our final destination. After all, what kind of crazy mouse would purposely visit a **VOLCANO**?

We hiked and hiked for seven days and seven nights. I was totally **wiped** out, but when we stopped to rest, I was tormented by terrible dreams. **SCARY** questions raced through my brain: What happened to Sproutness? Was she hurt? Could we save her?

I **tossed** and turned all night long and once I nearly **rolled** off the side of a cliff! I didn't want to tell the others I was having terrifying dreams about finding Sproutness. I mean, I was supposed to be a **BRAVE** and **courageous** knight! So, to explain all the rolling around, I told the others I was dreaming I was competing on the reality TV show *Scampering with the Stars*.

Finally, on the eighth day, at the base of a rocky valley, we spotted the unmistakable **Volcano of Fire**.

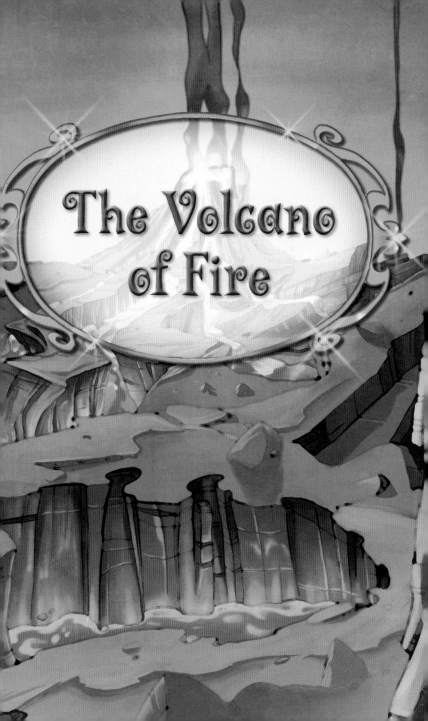

WELCOME TO THE VOLCANO OF FIRE!

The Gnomes of Fire live here. They are evil creatures who try to wake volcanoes and start earthquakes.

1. THE GREAT ABYSMAL FURNACE
2. MINOR FURNACES (REDHOTTIA, INFLAMEA, BURNNIA)
3. GREAT BOILER'S WAY
4. GREAT ASPHYXIATING SMOKE
5. LITTLE COUGH-CAUSING SMOKE
6. LITTLE STINKY PLUME
7. THE TRAIL OF THE ROASTED TRAVELER
8. BURNING-FEET PATH
9. SCALDING BREATH CRAG
10. SCARED TRAVELER'S ROCK
11. THE VOLCANO OF FIRE
12. REBOILED ABYSS

THE VOLCANO OF FIRE!

The volcano rose up from the ground, FIERCE
and imposing. Immediately, my fur stood on end.
Oh, how did I get myself into these situations? I
was **scared** out of my wits!

Then, as I looked closer, I realized something
even more frightening.

Plumes of SMOKE were spewing out of the
top of the volcano!

"That's strange," said Sterling. "The **Volcano of Fire** has been dormant for centuries. Smoke should not be coming out of its crater."

"That's not strange, that's deadly!" I shrieked, completely forgetting I was trying to act brave.

"RUN FOR YOUR LIFE!"

I tried to run, but Sterling grabbed me by the tail.

"It's okay, Knight," Sterling said soothingly. "It's okay to be **scared**. But we need to finish our mission. We need to find Sproutness and figure out what's setting off the earthquakes."

Run for your life!

I CHEWED my pawnails. "I-I-I'm n-n-not scared," I stammered. "I just thought maybe it might be a good idea to go for a RUN before we climb the volcano. You know, WARM up the muscles a little bit."

THUNDERHORN put a hand on my shoulder.

"Don't be embarrassed, Knight," he said. "It's normal to be AFRAID. Everyone gets scared, even the most courageous heroes. Even me, the King of the Elves. But like my old weapons teacher used to say, 'The real hero is not the one who is never afraid, but the one who has FEAR and is able to overcome it.'"

I REALIZED my friends were right. I'd have to face my fears and keep going. Well, not all of my fears. I mean, I was also afraid of

> **EVEN A HERO CAN BE SCARED SOMETIMES**
> It is normal to be scared in certain situations. Believe it or not, everyone gets scared at one time or another. A true hero is not someone who is never afraid, but someone who knows how to face his or her fears.

the **dark**, giant **SPIDERS**, and the recorded message on my dentist's answering machine . . . the background **drilling** noises creep me out!

Anyway, I took a deep breath as we continued through a dry, **ROCKY** valley. Here and there we passed puddles of **BOILING** mud that smelled like **sulfur**. And in the distance, we could see geysers shooting high into the air. I remembered reading about geysers in the Talking Library:

GEYSER: a spring of hot water that erupts periodically, sending forth columns of hot water and steam.

I sat down on a rock to check the map and said, "We're looking for some place called the **WHITE GIANT**."

I scratched my head. "Do you guys see any **GIANTS**?" I asked.

Then I heard a **ROAR** from under me. . . .

Suddenly I was lifted up into the air on a stream of **boiling** water and steam about thirty feet from the ground!

"Help!" I squeaked. "I'm afraid of heights!"

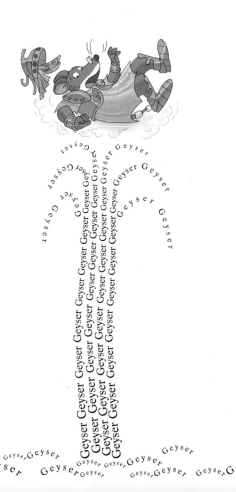

Oohhh!

As if it had heard me, the steamy water immediately stopped. I fell to the ground, **SMASHING** my tail on a pointy stone.

SMASH!

"Youch! You didn't have to drop me so *fast*!" I cried.

Once again, the geyser lifted me off the ground. Then it dropped me. Then it lifted me. Then it dropped me. UP. DOWN. UP. DOWN.

This geyser couldn't make up its mind!

Helppppp!

At last, Sterling **yanked** me off the geyser.

"You found the WHITE GIANT, Knight," Thunderhorn observed. "You were sitting on it!"

I rubbed my SORE tail and shot the geyser an EVIL

Youch!

look over my shoulder. It **gurgled** playfully, almost as if it were laughing at me. *Could this get any worse?* I thought. And then it did.

A second later, a terrible **earthquake** tremor shook the earth, throwing us to the ground.

We saved ourselves by hiding behind a **LARGE** rock.

"I want to live! I'm too fond of my fur!" I sobbed, squeezing my eyes shut. I was so busy crying, I didn't

realize the TREMOR had stopped until I felt someone gently tugging on my whisker.

"Um, Knight, you can get up now. The earthquake is over," said a voice. Slowly, I opened my eyes. It was Sterling.

Oh, how **HUMILIATING**!

I stood up and dusted off my fur. "Ahem, everybody ready?" I asked. Thunderhorn and Sterling nodded politely. I guess it was obvious that the only one *not* ready was me. "Okay, let's go!" I squeaked, trying to sound brave. Then I led the way down a rocky path.

I was just breathing in the fresh mountain air when suddenly we were hit with a strong wind carrying a cloud of GRAY ashes. Before long, we were CHOKING and covered in soot.

When we spotted a clear stream, Sterling took off her armor and jumped in to get clean.

"Girls . . ." Thunderhorn grumbled, until he

caught sight of his own **soot**-covered reflection. A minute later he, too, was in the water.

I decided to join them. But when I tried to pull off my tail cover, it got stuck.

I PULLED . . . and I PULLED . . . and I PULLED!

Finally, it popped off . . . but at the same time I accidentally **KiCKED** my bag into the water!

FIRST VOLUME
ENCYCLOPEDICUS
BOOKUS

As soon as the bag fell into the water, a little voice yelled out, "Help! Save me!"

I looked around, confused. Who had yelled that? Who needed help? It was just me, Sterling, and Thunderhorn. Not another soul in sight. I was beginning to think maybe I had taken too many rocks to the head during that last **tremor** when I heard the **SCREAM** again. This time it seemed farther away.

"**HELP! SAVE ME!**"

Only then did I realize that my bag was **FLOATING** away, carried by the strong current of the stream.

Was it possible that my **BAG** was **talking**?

Curious, I began to follow it. I ran along one edge of the **STREAM**, while Sterling and Thunderhorn tried to reach the bag from the other side.

When the bag hit a tiny **whirlpool**, I jumped in after it. Rats! The water was **cold**! But when I grabbed the bag, I was happy I had jumped in. There really was something moving around inside of my bag, and it was **shaking** with fright!

"Hang on! I will save you!" I yelled.

Careful!

I was congratulating myself on my heroic act when a strong current began pulling me downstream.

It was then that I noticed that Thunderhorn was flailing his arms, trying to get my attention. My heart filled with dread. What was he trying to tell me? I couldn't hear a thing. The water was so loud!

I tried desperately to read his lips:

Care — ful . . . of . . . the . . . wat — er — fall!

Waterfall?

A moment later I began to fall fall fall fall fall

"Tell me when it's over!" I wailed, closing my eyes. I ended up in the water below. I was alive! I grabbed on to a rock, but my bag was dragged away by the current.

"**HELP!**" the voice yelled again.

Whatever the voice belonged to, I needed to save it. If only I knew how.

Then I remembered the **medallion** and pulled it out.

"SAVE THAT BAG!"

I squeaked.

Immediately, an ORANGE RAY of light shot out of the medallion. It turned into a glowing net that grabbed the bag and brought it to shore.

I did my best mousey-**PADDLE** (did I mention I'm not the best swimmer in the pool?) and made it to the shore, too. When I opened the bag, something jumped out, **squeezed** my neck, and cried, "Thank you! Thank you, Knight! You saved my life! I will never forget this, ever! May my pages all rip out if I ever forget! I give my word, or my name isn't **First Volume Encyclopedicus Bookus**. Oh, but everyone calls me Vol for short."

It was a book from the Talking Library. After I **PEELED** him off of my neck, I asked, "What are you doing here?"

He shook his soaking pages, **stretched** out his **drenched** cover, and spluttered, "Um . . . I decided to come with you. I was **BORED** out of my spine, and it sounded like you were going on a fun adventure. So I got in your bag."

First Volume Encyclopedicus Bookus

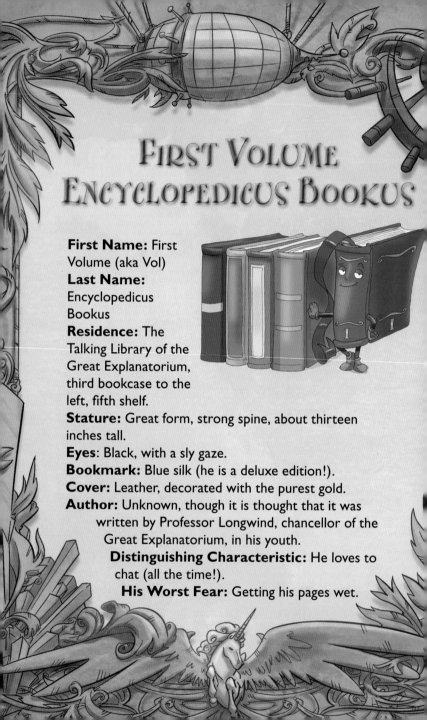

First Name: First Volume (aka Vol)

Last Name: Encyclopedicus Bookus

Residence: The Talking Library of the Great Explanatorium, third bookcase to the left, fifth shelf.

Stature: Great form, strong spine, about thirteen inches tall.

Eyes: Black, with a sly gaze.

Bookmark: Blue silk (he is a deluxe edition!).

Cover: Leather, decorated with the purest gold.

Author: Unknown, though it is thought that it was written by Professor Longwind, chancellor of the Great Explanatorium, in his youth.

Distinguishing Characteristic: He loves to chat (all the time!).

His Worst Fear: Getting his pages wet.

A fun adventure? This mission was turning into a scary nightmare. But what could I do now? I couldn't leave the talking book behind to fend for himself. He might fall into the water again or get SQUASHED by a falling boulder.

"Okay, Vol," I said, placing the book on a rock to dry. "You can come with us."

"Yes!" he squealed happily, ruffling his pages in the sun.

Yes!

THE BAD NEWS IS . . .

While Vol was drying out, I looked around. I was on the shore of a stream that ran down to a narrow and **DEEP** valley.

We were getting closer and closer to the **Volcano of Fire**!

I emptied my bag and laid everything out to dry. My change of clothes, the map of the Kingdom of Fantasy, and Sproutness's precious **medallion**.

I looked at it closely. The orange stone had lost its color and turned **gray**. I shivered. Don't get me wrong, I was happy I had used it to save Vol, but now there were only five wishes left!

After a few minutes, Thunderhorn and Sterling found us sitting by the water's edge. They **WRAPPED** me up in a group hug, happy to see I was okay. Then I introduced them to the newest member of our group. Vol was so excited he immediately began **JUMPING** up and down like my great-grandmother Sandyfur when she wins bingo night at the Resting Rats Retirement Village.

Long live the knight!

For the next twenty hours (or was it twenty minutes?), he babbled on and on about how I had rescued him, how he always wanted to become an **ADVENTURE** book, and blah blah blah.

By the time the book stopped talking, I was ready for a nice **long** nap. Too bad we had no time for naps. We had to get to that volcano.

Thunderhorn had been studying the map, and

said he had some GOOD news. "We are at the base of the **Volcano of Fire**," he announced.

"Hooray!" I cried.

Then he continued. "The **bad** news is, we have to climb up to the top of the volcano to figure out what is going on."

I looked at the really tall and REALLY STEEP walls of rock that made up the volcano.

"Climb these walls?" I gulped. Just looking at them was giving me  vertigo

Seeing that I was about to pass out, Vol began **fanning** me with his pages. He climbed onto my back.

"Don't be **afraid**, Knight!" the talking book said. "I will help you!"

My head was **spinning** as I began to climb.

"Don't look down," Vol advised. "Actually, I have an idea. I will just cover your eyes." So he did.

Then I took a deep breath, gathered my strength, and pulled myself up the STEEP rocky wall. After what seemed like forever, Vol uncovered my eyes. "You did it!" he cheered.

We had reached the top of the VOLCANO!

Come on, Knight!

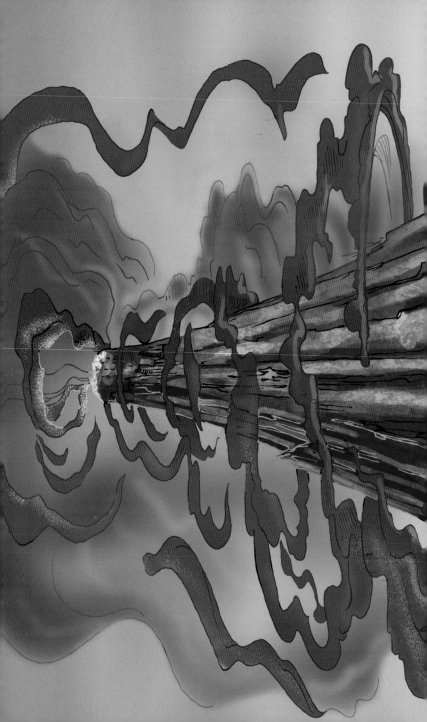

THE VOLCANO OF FIRE

The Volcano of Fire is the tallest volcano in the Kingdom of Fantasy and lies west of the Kingdom of the Elves. For many centuries, the volcano was dormant, but now streams of smoke pour out of its crater regularly. The erupting volcano has led to terrible earthquakes, which have been destroying the Kingdom of Fantasy.

A THOUSAND EVIL GNOMES OF FIRE!

We knelt before the crater of the volcano. It was a big, **DARK**, gaping hole. *Swirls* of black **stinky** smoke rose into the air from somewhere deep inside the crater.

"I wonder what's causing all this **stinky** smoke," Princess Sterling whispered.

I was thinking the same thing. I poked my head over the edge of the crater and looked down.

Shhh!

The hole was really deep, but somewhere way down at the bottom of the volcano I thought I could see something moving.

What could it be? I tried squinting. I tried cleaning my glasses. But I still couldn't make out what the something was within all the smoke.

"I can't see a thing!" Vol complained.

"SHHH!" I warned the talking book.

Then Thunderhorn leaned over the crater and whispered, "There is someone down there. I can see them with my acute ELF VISION, and . . ."

Suddenly, he jumped back. "I don't believe it!" he cried. "There are a thousand evil gnomes with beards as RED as FIRE down there, and they are throwing trees into the mouth of the volcano!"

"Trees?" I asked.

"Yes," Thunderhorn went on, his face growing PALE. "And the worst part of all is that the trees are from our precious elfin forest!"

Rancid rat hairs! We had to do something!

We huddled together, whispering softly. There were lots of questions we needed to answer. Such as: Who were these **EVIL** gnomes? Why were they **BURNING** the elves' trees? Was what they were doing causing the earthquakes?

Oh, where was a computer with **Internet** to search when you needed one?

Just then, Vol **FLAPPED** his bookmark, and whispered importantly, "I will search my pages. I don't mean to brag, but let me just say that I know a lot. **TONS**. In fact, I know almost everything there is to know, and . . ."

Luckily, Sterling interrupted him before he went on.

"No offense, but could you just get the **INFO**?" she pleaded.

"Okay, okay," Vol huffed. "Here we go, under *G* for *gnomes*: Gnomes of the

THE GNOMES OF FIRE

 he Gnomes of Fire are found in the mouths of dormant volcanoes, where they live off of ashes and lava. They love fire and darkness, but most of all they love waking volcanoes from their slumber. That is why they build enormous furnaces in the craters of volcanoes, where they light fires and play gigantic drums that are terribly loud.

The Gnomes of Fire are governed by His Burning Majesty, King Griller IV of the ancient line of Gnomes of Fire. He is known as Lord of the Burners, Master of Greatlava, Sire of the Hot Heads, and the Great Incinerator. His wife is Queen Charcoalrella III of the Sulfur dynasty, also known as Lady Flaminglava.

The gnomes are very dangerous creatures because they have bad tempers. The only thing they fear is water.

Field . . . GNOMES OF FIRE!"

Quickly, we read the information.

I shuddered. This mission was getting scarier by the minute! It was bad enough we were sitting at the top of a BURNING-HOT volcano, but now we had to worry about evil gnomes.

SHOCKED by what we had just learned about the gnomes, we sat on the ground next to the crater to figure out a plan.

I was all for crying hysterically for the next twenty minutes, but I had a feeling no one would go for that idea, so I kept silent.

"We can't just attack," Sterling reasoned. "There are a thousand gnomes and only four of us."

Meanwhile, Thunderhorn drew some designs in the dirt. "Hmmm, the only thing the Gnomes of Fire are afraid of is water. . . ." he muttered softly. Then he snapped his fingers. "I've got it!" he exclaimed. "We need water! Lots and lots of it! The **wateR** will scare the gnomes and put out the FIRE in the volcano!"

"But where are we going to find **wateR**?" I asked anxiously.

Thunderhorn continued, "I know someone who knows a lot about **wateR**. His name is Captain Coldheart. He is the terrible captain of the flying ship *The Bronze Anchor* and leader of the Coldheart Gang, the pirates who travel the skies, capturing LIGHTNING bolts and causing storms. Everyone is afraid of them in the Kingdom of Fantasy."

"Are you sure he can help?" Sterling asked doubtfully.

"Coldheart owes me a favor. He will help," Thunderhorn said.

I was wondering how you would go about finding a ship that FLIES when Sterling jumped to her feet.

"I will handle this!" she announced.

Then she played her silver flute. Immediately, her dragon Sparkle appeared. Together they disappeared into the clouds.

At dawn the next day we were awakened by a powerful yell: "Throw the anchor!"

A second later, an enormouse bronze anchor nearly chopped off my tail! Ack!

The Coldheart Gang had arrived!

Ack!

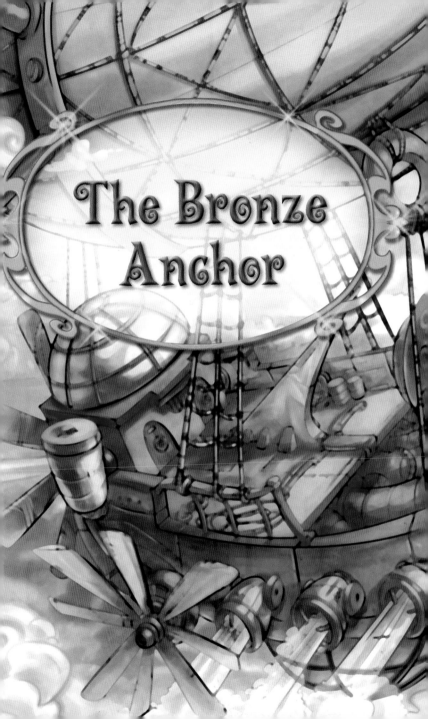

The Bronze Anchor

WELCOME ABOARD *THE BRONZE ANCHOR!*

It is a pirate ship, the terror of the skies and the bringer of wind, hail, and storms!

1. THE GREAT FLYING BALLOON (NOT AVAILABLE FOR BIRTHDAY PARTIES)
2. THE MAJOR PROPELLER ON THE STERN
3. THE MINOR CLOUD CHOPPER PROPELLER
4. FRESH LIGHTNING BOLT RESERVE
5. THE QUARTERS OF CAPTAIN COLDHEART
6. WIND-CUTTING FIN
7. ICE-BLENDING MACHINE
8. LIGHTNING-GRABBER WINGS
9. WIND-BLOWER MASTHEAD
10. LIGHTNING-SHOOTER ANTENNA
11. THE GREAT SHOWER (SHOOTS OUT DOWNPOURS OF THE HIGHEST QUALITY!)

BUUAAHAHA!
BUUAAHAHA!
BUUAAHAHA!

Before I could even let out a squeak, a voice like thunder screamed, "Creeeewww! Let the guests on board!"

Then it broke out in a deep, CREEPY laugh that sent chills down my fur. "Buuaahaha! Buuaahaha! Buuaahaha!"

I cringed. It had to be Captain Coldheart. Something told me he wasn't exactly the warm and fuzzy type.

"Uh, are you SURE about this?" I asked Thunderhorn as a hundred voices shouted, "Yes, Captain! Right away, Captain!"

Before Thunderhorn could reply, a rope ladder was thrown down, and we CLIMBED aboard the old and rusty **floating** ship.

Luckily, the climb didn't take too long, but when we reached the deck, I wished that it had taken longer. We were surrounded by a crew of **MONSTERS** more **HIDEOUS** than I could ever imagine!

Shuddering, I stared at the scary monsters.

There were:

★ **75** Octoslimes — *creatures with octopus heads and tentacles dripping with* slime

★ **93** Stinkshells — *monsters with bodies like black mussel shells who give off a terrible* STINK

★ **67** Boulderbrains — *dimwitted creatures with bodies made entirely of* ROCKS

★ **362** Spidezillas — *spiderlike monsters with eight hairy legs and sharp yellow* FANGS

★ Many other creatures whose HIDEOUS faces I will never forget!

In front of all of them stood Captain Coldheart. "WELCOME ABOARD *THE BRONZE ANCHOR*!" he sneered.

I don't know what I was EXPECTING from a captain whose last name was Coldheart. HUGS all around? A plate of freshly baked COOKIES?

Not a chance!

Octoslimes

STINKSHELLS

BOULDERBRAINS

SPIDEZILLAS

The captain looked us up and down with **ANGRY** eyes, then ordered his crew to throw us in the ship's prison. "Your little friend Sterling will be happy to see you!" he chuckled darkly.

"Um, but, sir . . ." I tried to explain.

He interrupted me, "You, the mousey one . . . you must be that brave knight, **GERONIMO OF STILTON** or whatever. Stop the squeaking!" Then he yelled, "Throw them in the **DARK HOLE**!"

I tried to explain again that we were on an

Um, Captain, sir . . .

URGENT mission that would affect the entire Kingdom of Fantasy, but the captain refused to listen.

Instead, he **STOMPED** his foot and shrieked. "Enough with the chatter!"

The next thing I knew, a hundred spider legs grabbed us, a hundred tentacles trapped us, and a hundred stone arms threw us into a *dark* and stinky prison.

There, curled up in a corner, was Sterling.

When she saw us, she jumped up. "Your plan didn't work, Thunderhorn! You said that Captain Coldheart would help us, but as soon as he saw me, he threw me in here!" she cried. "Luckily, my dragon Sparkle was able to escape!"

Thunderhorn smiled mysteriously. "Don't be so quick to judge, Princess," he insisted in a soft voice. "The captain is known throughout the Kingdom of Fantasy for being terribly

FEROCIOUS, but he is also very loyal. He never forgets to return a favor. Just wait. You'll see."

"Loyalty shmoyalty!" Sterling huffed. "You've really done it this time, Thunderhorn. We should **NEVER** have listened to you. Just because you're an **elf king** doesn't mean you know everything!"

Then she turned her back to Thunderhorn and didn't say another word.

Thunderhorn crossed his arms over his chest. He **whirled** around and faced the other way, sulking.

"Don't **FIGHT**, you two," I said.

Even Vol tried to help. He flipped through his pages until he reached the definition of *quarrel*. "Here it is: 'useless bickering that has no purpose and does not solve problems . . .'" he read aloud.

But the two didn't budge.

How were we going to fight the **bad guys** when we were fighting among ourselves?

GOOD LUCK, SPIES!

The next morning, two octoslimes came to get us, grabbing us with their **slimy** tentacles. They had so many tentacles that it only took two of them to **tie** all of us up and **CARRY** us away.

They took us to Captain Coldheart's quarters to be interrogated.

Oh, what a nightmare!

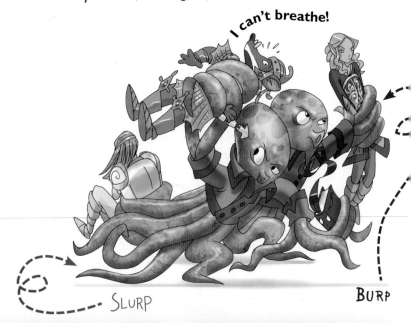

I can't breathe!

SLURP

BURP

The octoslimes opened the door and flung us into the room like they were throwing out bags of **rotting** trash. How insulting!

"Good luck with the captain, you evil **SPIES**!" they snarled. "You're gonna need it!"

The captain greeted us with a **menacing** look. "Well done, **Slurp**. Well done, **Burp**," he praised the octoslimes. "I'll take care of these lowlifes!"

One of the octoslimes **belched** loudly as they both left. I'd bet my left paw he was the one named **Burp**!

I turned to Captain Coldheart. By now, my whiskers were shaking with fear. I could only imagine what the evil captain had in store for us "spies," and none of it was good. Would he make us walk the **PLANK**? Would he drop us off on a cloud in the middle of nowhere? Would he force us to eat cheesecake without the **cheese**?

But, strangely, nothing bad happened.

Instead, the captain did three things: **(1)** First, he poked his head out of the door to make sure that no one was **spying** on us. **(2)** Then he turned on an old record player that played terrible screams. It was like the soundtrack to a **HORROR** film. **(3)** Finally, he pushed a button that was hidden under his desk.

We heard a **rumble**, and suddenly, comfortable armchairs rose **up** from the wooden floor. With another **rumble**, a small table covered with a tablecloth and plates filled with delicious pastries popped up. Yum!

There was even a porcelain ᴛᴇᴀ ꜱᴇᴛ and cups for every guest!

"Make yourselves nice and comfortable," said the captain. "And don't look so surprised. I know this all seems a **little fishy**, but I will explain. . . .

"You see, everyone thinks I'm **mean** and **CRUEL**, and they have to keep thinking that, or I'm in **BIG** trouble. You won't tell on me, right?"

We promised we wouldn't tell anyone, and the captain continued.

"Now I will tell you my strange story. I was born into a family of pirates. My dad was a

Make yourselves comfortable!

PIRATE. My mom was a **PIRATE**. I had little **PIRATE** brothers and sisters. But I never felt as if I belonged because, well, you see, I am too much of a **softy** to be a pirate."

At this, he **BURST** into tears. "Oh, what a tragedy! I have to force myself to pretend to be mean just to fit in. The only time I can be myself is when I'm with friends, like you," he went on. "That's why you can't tell anyone. If my **monsters** knew the truth, they wouldn't listen to me, and I'd be unemployed."

Then he sighed. "So that's me in a nutshell. Anyway, I'd **LOVE** to keep chatting, but I've got work to do. About thirty miles from here, there is an island where it hasn't rained in months. The poor creatures who live there are starving because their land is dried out and nothing is growing anymore. . . ."

"We don't want to get in the way of your work,

CAPTAIN COLDHEART

Captain Coldheart comes from a long line of ruthless pirates. Not wanting to embarrass his family, he pretends to be ruthless, but actually he has a heart as soft as Brie! He travels on his flying ship, *The Bronze Anchor*. His crew is made up of terrible monsters that believe him to be an extremely cruel pirate. Together, they travel the skies and capture lightning bolts.

Captain Coldheart runs the ship and directs it to places around the Kingdom of Fantasy where it has not rained in a while, and he causes storms, to bring water where there isn't any . . . but don't tell anyone! His kindness must be kept secret!

Uhmmm...

Captain," Thunderhorn said. "But we were wondering if you might be able to help us out with a **MISSION** of our own."

The pirate, who had just shoved two cookies in his mouth, mumbled, "Mission?"

Thunderhorn explained that we needed to extinguish the great **BONFIRE** that the Gnomes of Fire had lit in the heart of the Volcano of Fire.

"We think the gnomes are involved in causing the **earthquakes**. Plus, they may have kidnapped our friend Princess Sproutness, the sister of Blossom, the Queen of the Fairies," Sterling added.

The Captain brushed cookie **crumbs** out of his mustache, then he said, "Well, of course I'll help. I never forget when I owe a friend a favor."

Thunderhorn shot Sterling a **LOOK**. "Was I right or was I right?" he whispered under his breath. But she just **ROLLED** her eyes. I guess she wasn't ready to let him off the hook yet.

Meanwhile, the captain came up with a plan. "I know!" he said. "I can position my boat right over the Volcano of Fire. Then I'll start a **STORM**, and the **rain** will put out the **FIRE**."

It sounded like a good idea at first, until we remembered about Princess Sproutness. If she was being held prisoner in the volcano, she might get **HURT**.

But Captain Coldheart shook his head at us.

Was I right or was I right?

Whatever!

"Sproutness isn't at the **volcano**," he said. "I'm almost positive."

He explained that one night he had spotted some **SUSPICIOUS CREATURES** carrying a young maiden. They took her west, past the volcano.

"I wanted to help, but my ship couldn't move. There was no **WIND**. Oh, what a tragedy!" the captain *wailed*, bursting into tears. It took a few **cookies** to make him feel better. Being a gentlemouse, I **crunched** on a few more myself. After all, no one likes to eat alone.

I was happily **CHEWING** my second cookie (okay, maybe it was my third, but who's counting) when Thunderhorn said, "I have an idea. After the captain puts out the fire in the volcano, we'll go down and check things out."

Check out the **INSIDE** of a volcano? How did I get myself into these situations? I just hoped I would live to tell about it!

The Captain explained that he was going to pretend to be **evil** again. He pressed the button, and everything disappeared: the chairs, the table, even the cookies. **Rats!**

Then he turned off the SCARY music. Finally, he opened the door of his quarters and bellowed:

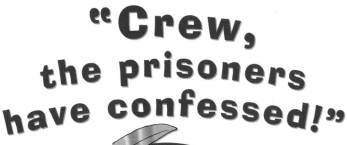

"Crew, the prisoners have confessed!"

HEAVE-HO!

The two octoslimes returned, grabbed us with their **SLIMY** tentacles, and dragged us to the deck, where the whole crew was waiting.

I have to say, Captain Coldheart really did look menacing. I almost forgot he was acting!

Immediately, the pirate monsters yelled, **"Long live the captain! All hail Captain Coldheart, the terror of the skies!"**

Then they began to sing a horrendous song and

Sheldon

Brutely

Slurp

Snap

shake their claws and hairy paws:

WE ARE SCARY MONSTERS!
WE'RE BAD TO THE CORE!
WE'LL CHEW YOU UP,
AND SPIT YOU OUT,
THEN SEND YOU SCREAMING
OUT THE DOOR!

OUR CAPTAIN IS OUR HERO,
HIS HEART'S MADE OUT OF ICE!
HE'S MEAN AND RUDE
AND CRUEL AND CRUDE!
IF YOU WANT TO MESS WITH HIM,
YOU'D BETTER THINK TWICE!

Hairy Legs   Hooks   Squawker

When the monsters finished singing, the captain ordered the crew to position the ship over the volcano and start the **storm** machines.

"I want **lightning**, hail, **RAIN**, the works!" the captain shrieked with an evil laugh.

This made the monsters so happy, they ran around the deck singing, "Long live Captain Coldheart!"

I had to give it to the captain. He really did make a great villain. Maybe he was in the drama club in **Pirate School**.

Just then I realized Vol was **trembling**. Didn't he get the memo? *It's just an act*, I wanted to tell him. But before I could reassure the talking book, he fainted, **SQUISHING** my tail in the process. Youch!

A minute later, the storm began. Thunder, LIGHTNING, hail, and rain poured down onto the volcano. The ship SWAYED back and forth, and I felt myself getting SEASICK . . . I mean airsick . . . I mean . . . well, you know what I mean. I felt ill.

But I had to keep going. We needed to search the volcano for Sproutness.

As we climbed down a long rope ladder, I tried to keep my wailing to a minimum.

Finally, we stood on the crater. I poked my head inside and saw that there was no longer any fire. The rain had put it out.

The storm had also scared away the GNOMES OF FIRE. We caught sight of them fleeing toward their secret underground tunnels.

A little while later, *The Bronze Anchor* **sailed** away, disappearing among the clouds. I wished we could have thanked Captain Coldheart, but we didn't want to blow his cover.

Just then, a shimmering **rainbow** appeared in the sky. Could it be a sign from the captain? I had no idea, but I did know one thing: It was beautiful!

I LOVE RAINBOWS!

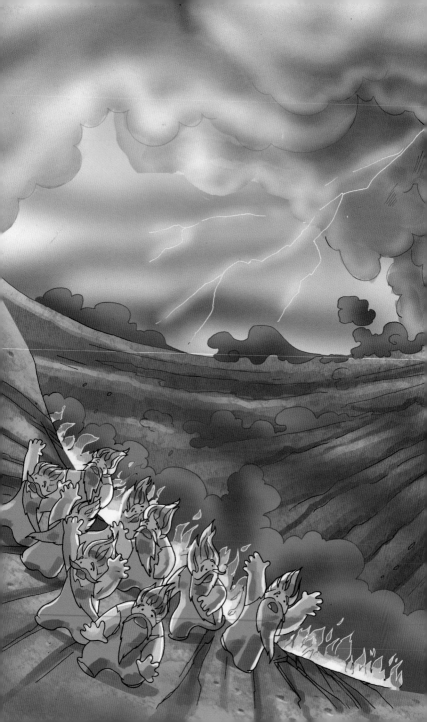

Reluctantly, I left the rainbow behind and followed everyone down to the bottom of the crater. Oh, how **SPOOKY**! We searched everywhere, but there was no sign of Sproutness. Maybe the captain was right, and she had been taken much farther west. But **WHO** had taken her? And **why**?

While we were deciding where to look next, disaster struck. The ground began to **rumble**. It was another earthquake tremor! I was so scared, I **SQUEEZED** my eyes shut. The fire was out, and the gnomes had fled, so why was the earth still **shaking**?

When I opened my eyes again, I saw something even scarier. Thunderhorn and Sterling were tumbling into a **GAPING** hole!

Immediately, I found the charmed medallion and shouted,

"SAVE MY FRIENDS!"

A **YELLOW RAY** shot out of the medallion, wrapped around them, and carried them to safety.

That was the good news. The bad news was that a moment later, I got hit on the head with a rock, and I **FAINTED**.

Suddenly, I found myself in a **DARK**, **DARK** tunnel. I couldn't even see my own paw in front of my face! Rancid rat hairs! Did I mention I'm afraid of the dark? Just when I thought I'd be trapped there forever, I spotted a marvelous **BLUE** light at the end of the tunnel. . . .

When I arrived at the end, I opened my eyes and . . . woke up!

I looked around. I was in a room made of **BLUE** crystal, stretched out on a **BLUE** bed and covered by a **BLUE** comforter.

Where was I? When I looked out the window I knew the place.

I was in **BLUE HORN**, the city of the **Blue Unicorns!**

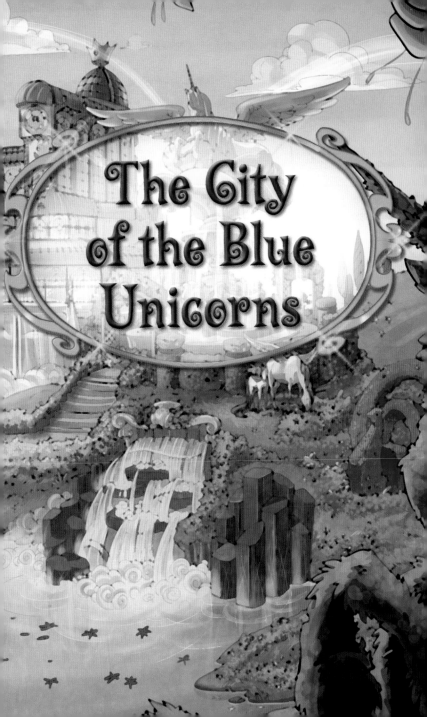

The City of the Blue Unicorns

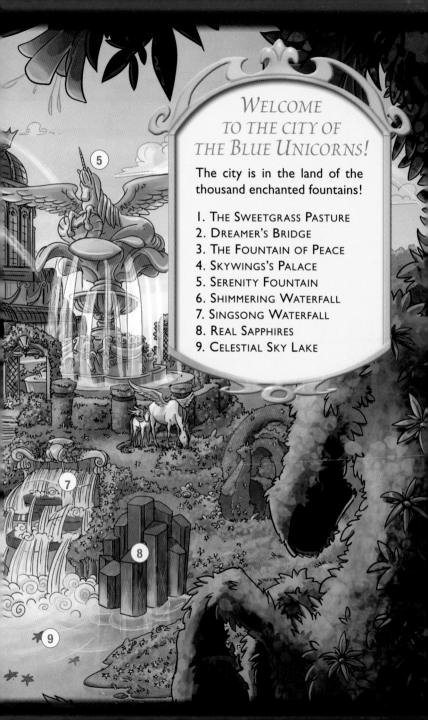

WELCOME TO THE CITY OF THE BLUE UNICORNS!

The city is in the land of the thousand enchanted fountains!

1. THE SWEETGRASS PASTURE
2. DREAMER'S BRIDGE
3. THE FOUNTAIN OF PEACE
4. SKYWINGS'S PALACE
5. SERENITY FOUNTAIN
6. SHIMMERING WATERFALL
7. SINGSONG WATERFALL
8. REAL SAPPHIRES
9. CELESTIAL SKY LAKE

TELL ME EVERYTHING!

I was admiring the incredible view of **BLUE HORN**, the city of the Blue Unicorns, when the door to my room burst open and my friends Thunderhorn, Sterling, Vol, and Captain Coldheart came in. We had a warm group hug. Then everyone began talking at once.

How are you?

I'm glad you're up!

"Hooray!"

"Finally, you woke up, Knight!"

"We were so worried!"

"Welcome back, matey!"

Welcome b.

As soon as I could squeak, I said, "What happened? Tell me **eVeRYtHiNG**!"

So they did. Sterling told me how I had saved her and

Thunderhorn when the earthquake **tremors** started in the volcano. "You used the medallion, remember?" she asked.

To be honest, I didn't remember, so I checked the medallion and saw that it was true. Now there were three **GRAY** stones because I had used the third wish.

"Knight, you should have been there! Well, you *were* there, but take my word for it — you were a **hero** with a capital **H**!" Vol exclaimed.

I scratched my head. "If you say so," I mumbled.

Thunderhorn smiled at me. "To save us, you fell into the hole and **HIT** your head. You were passed out for three days and three nights," he continued.

Ouch!

"I had to **fish** you out from the bottom of the hole," Captain Coldheart added. "I used a small anchor to do it. And I'm sorry I

HERE'S WHAT HAPPENED AFTER I FAINTED:

I fell into the hole and hit my head.

Captain Coldheart came to fish me out....

...he dragged me up by the tail!

My friends took me to Blue Horn.

scratched your tail. . . ."

I turned around and realized that my tail was bandaged. **HUH?** I looked in the mirror and squeaked. Most of the rest of me was bandaged, too. I looked just like a **mummy**!

"After fishing you out, we took you here. The **Blue Unicorns** are the best **healers** in all of the Kingdom of Fantasy," Sterling explained.

Huh?

"They sure are!" **VOL** piped up. "I know all about them because I know everything and guess what, Knight, you were seen by the King of the Unicorns himself. What an honor, I mean . . ."

Vol yammered on and on until **Quicksilver**, a unicorn of the court, appeared and announced,

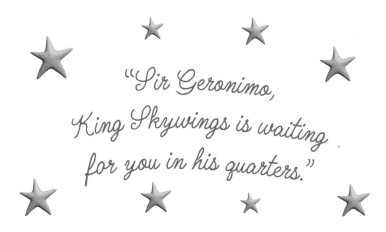

"Sir Geronimo, King Skywings is waiting for you in his quarters."

WHY ARE YOU FOLLOWING ME?

After Thunderhorn and Sterling left, I got ready to meet the King.

Vol stayed behind. He insisted that I read about the Blue Unicorns and the court **etiquette**.

"You don't want to make a **FOOL** of yourself," he said, **FLIPPING** through his pages. "Not that you would, of course, but still . . ."

He blabbed on about this and that until he got to the page he was looking for. "Here, **read** this," he instructed.

I wanted to make a good impression on the king, so I was careful to **WASH** up, **BRUSH** my fur, and polish my armor until it sparkled. But when I

Here, read this!

KING SKYWINGS OF
THE BLUE MANE GROUP

ise King Skywings, sire of the Unicorns, of the noble dynasty of Blue Manes, Lord of the Trade Winds and Keeper of the Great Blue Sapphires, rules Blue Horn, the city of the Blue Unicorns. He is the keeper of the precious secret of the Unicorns, which is (Shhh! Don't tell anyone) that their fountains are capable of healing every wound of the body and the heart.

Alas, the Kingdom of the Unicorns does not have a queen. King Skywings is still looking for that special filly with whom he can share his apples and carrots.

As a sign of respect for their king, the subjects attend the Royal Hearings with their manes brushed and their fur shined. They bow three times before they leave the throne room, and then they walk backward so they do not turn their backs on His Majesty.

tried to put my armor back on, my tail got stuck because of all the bandages. Rats! If I didn't take my bandages off, I'd have to stand in front of the king in my **nightshirt**! How mortifying!

Vol offered to help me. He grabbed the edge of my tail bandage and began pulling, **spinning** himself around and around. In a few seconds, he was completely **WRAPPED** up!

"**HELP**, get me out of here!" he cried. "I've mummified myself!"

He had **wrapped** himself up so tightly that it took me half an hour to untangle him. And that made

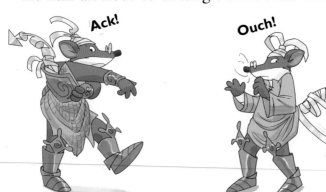

Ack!

Ouch!

I'll do it!

I tried to put on my armor, but my tail got stuck.

Then Vol offered to help take the bandages off my tail . . .

me late to meet the king!

I quickly put my armor on and *darted* out of the room with Vol right on my tail.

. . . and in a few seconds, he was totally wrapped up!

"Why are you following me?" I asked. Who would have thought a book could be so annoying?

"Because I need to take notes! If I really want to become an adventure book, I can't miss anything that is happening in this story!" he said.

What could I say? I allowed him to accompany me to the royal pavilion, but I made him promise to wait outside and not cause any TROUBLE.

Vol put his hands on his cover, clearly offended. "You know, Knight, I am not a BRAND-NEW book, fresh off the press! I know how to handle myself, okay? I'm telling you straight, in black ink. And if that's not enough, I will tell you in **bold**, in *italics*, and even in CAPITAL LETTERS!"

"Okay," I nodded, hoping the book was good for his word.

We took off for the **royal pavilion** and soon stood before the entrance to King Skywings's chambers. Nervously, I gave one last **SHINE** to my armor. "Wish me luck," I said to Vol, but when I looked down, he had disappeared.

The king greeted me with a flap of his **BLUE** wings. Bowing before him, I thanked him for saving my life.

"I'm glad to see you are feeling better," replied the king. "And now I would like to help you with your mission. Listen closely, and I will reveal to you the **secret** of the Blue Unicorns. . . ."

But before the king could continue, all of a sudden there was a loud sneeze from behind a pair

of heavy window curtains. *ACHOO!*

I moved the curtains, and there stood Vol! So much for telling it straight in **CAPITAL LETTERS**!

"Excuse me, I was just **LOOKING** for my bookmark, Your **Blueness**, I mean Lord Skytail, I mean King Skywings . . ." Vol stammered.

The king looked at the book as if he were from the **SCIENCE-FICTION** section.

"Well, um, I've got to run," Vol mumbled, **HOPPING** off.

Oh, why was that book always trying to get me into *TROUBLE*?

Luckily, the king didn't ask me any questions. Instead, he waited for Vol to leave, then said, "Follow me, Knight, and I will show you that **SECRET**. . . ."

The king **TROTTED** out of the royal pavilion and into the field.

I did my best to keep up, but I was soon *gasping* for breath. "Your Majesty, wait for me . . ." I huffed. But he didn't hear me.

Your Majesty, wait for me!

Holey cheese, that unicorn could move!

As I stumbled through a big field with the GREENEST GRASS, I accidentally slammed into a pole with lots of signs on it. I ended up snoutdown in the field.

How embarrassing!

I tried frantically to put all of the signs back onto the pole, but I didn't know where they went. So I put them all back **randomly**.

THE SECRET OF
THE UNICORNS

While I put the signs back, I noticed that the names were really **strange**:

The Fountain of Youth,

The Fountain of Love,

The Fountain of Oblivion,

The Fountain of MEMORiES,

The Fountain of Strength,

The Fountain of HEALTH,

The Fountain of Courage,

The Fountain of WISDOM,

The Fountain of Truth . . . and many others!

Who knew if I had put them back correctly?

But there was no time to worry about it. KING SKYWINGS was already far ahead of me, and I had to catch up.

Right then, I saw Thunderhorn and Sterling.

They were practicing their fencing moves while standing on the narrow **STONE** edge of a beautiful gold **FOUNTAIN** of water that had a heart at the top of it.

They moved quickly, as if they were **DANCING**. I was amazed at how they were able to keep their balance while they practiced. I had trouble talking while standing on one paw!

The two were concentrating so hard, they didn't even notice me.

"Hi, guys!" I squeaked when I approached.

At the sound of my voice, Thunderhorn and Sterling lost their concentration and their balance. For a minute, they waved their arms in the air, then they both fell into the fountain with a loud **SPLASH**!

"Sorry!" I apologized. But neither noticed.

Instead, they were staring at each other with the **strangest** expression in their eyes. . . .

CAN YOU GUESS WHICH FOUNTAIN THIS IS?

Hint:
It has to do with matters of the heart

I left Sterling and Thunderhorn in the fountain (who knew what had gotten into them) and continued on my way. At long last, I caught up with King Skywings. I was so exhausted, I was **HUFFING** like the Rodent Express train.

I stumbled up to the unicorn's side. He was **chattering** away.

"Um, sorry, Your Majesty," I huffed. "But I'm afraid I didn't hear you."

King Skywings just kept right on talking.

"And now I will reveal our most precious **SECRET** to you. . . ." he announced. *At least I didn't miss the good part*, I thought as the king continued, lowering his voice. "The secret of the **Blue Unicorns** is the fountains from which we get water for our healing potions. Each fountain has a particular property. Some give

STRENGTH, others courage, others help us forget, others help us remember, and some allow us to see our true **love** . . . but you must be careful to give everyone the right **water**, in the right quantity, otherwise you can cause problems."

I was thinking about the fountain Sterling and Thunderhorn had fallen into when the king instructed me to follow him.

"Knight, I want you to look into the Fountain of **TRUTH**. It can show hidden truths to those who are worthy. It might help with your mission."

He led me to a stone basin, on which there was an inscription in the Fantasian alphabet:

Are you able to translate it?*

* You can find the Fantasian alphabet on page 310.

King Skywings translated the inscription for me. It said *Look and Learn*.

Then he urged me to go ahead and look into the fountain. My heart was pounding. I wasn't sure I wanted to know the **TRUTH**. What if it was something bad? What if I found out Sproutness was hurt? What if Vol was really a **spy**? What if I found a gray whisker?

I stared into the **fountain**, feeling like I was about to faint. At first, I didn't see a thing. Then the king stirred up the water with his horn.

When the water had calmed, images began to form. My eyes opened wide. Who were those strange creatures?

THE DIGGERTS

I rubbed my eyes, but when I looked again, the **creatures** were still there. They had **LONG** beards, bushy **eyebrows**, and were dressed in earthy colors. Each one carried a heavy bag of **ROCKS**.

They seemed to be walking in some sort of dark underground tunnel. Smoke **whirled** up in streams all around them.

I was still trying to get a good look at these bizarre creatures when the image CLOUDED over. A second later, another image formed in the reflection of the water.

I saw a girl tied up, trying to get free, while the earth shook around her. Then I realized it was Sproutness! She was being held prisoner!

Sproutness!

We needed to help her, and fast! She looked so sad and weak.

After the images in the water vanished, we headed back to the palace. As we walked, I asked the king all of the questions that had been swirling around in my brain, such as: WHERE was Sproutness being held? WHO were those strange creatures in the tunnel?

King Skywings did his best to answer my questions. Unfortunately, he didn't recognize

 the place where Sproutness was being held prisoner, but he did know a little about the **bizarre** creatures. They were known as **Diggerts**, and they worked as miners.

"They're not dangerous, and the thing they love most is digging and hauling rocks in their mines," the unicorn explained. "The **Diggerts** are also famous for singing beautiful *songs* while they work. It is believed that their *songs* soften the stones, making their work easier."

I scratched my head. The creatures in the image hadn't exactly look like they were **JUMPING** for joy. And instead of singing, they had looked like they were all grumbling.

I didn't understand one bit about what was going on. But at least I was sure of one thing: We needed to rescue SPROUTNESS.

The king convinced us to wait until the morning

before we set off. "It's too **DANGEROUS** to travel at night," he insisted. "Plus, it will give me a chance to put together some special hiking equipment, clothes, and anything else you might need for your journey. And besides, I would like to treat you to a **MOUTHWATERING** four-course good-bye banquet."

Did someone say **MOUTHWATERING** banquet?! Immediately, I began to **DROOL**. I eagerly accepted the king's invitation. I mean, I was very glad the king had offered to replace all of the hiking equipment we had lost in the waterfall. But the thought of a delicious meal made my stomach do a happy dance. I was **STARVING**!

The king galloped ahead, and by the time I reached the **royal pavilion**, a banquet table had been set.

I couldn't wait to **DIG** in! But when I saw the food, I gasped.

There were **golden** dishes in the shape of troughs that were filled with *hay*, along with jugs of herbal water and plates of clovers and flowers! Where was the cheese?

King Skywings offered me a plate filled with bright *blue* flowers.

"Have some *bluespearia*, Knight," he

Bon appétit, Knight!

What a strange menu!

It smells great!

said. "It's a delicacy here in Blue Horn. These flowers give our coats our blue color."

Would they make me a mouse with blue fur?

I didn't want to insult the king, but I had to pass on the *bluespearia*. In fact, I wanted

I'm starved!

I'm so hungry!

Yum!

Burp!

Ack!

to pass on the whole meal. It was terrible!

The hay was impossible to **chew** and kept getting stuck in between my teeth. I could tell Sterling and the captain felt the same way about it.

I'm chewing...
and chewing...

The **ONLY** one who I saw enjoying himself was Thunderhorn. I wasn't too surprised. He had spent so many years as a **deer**, he was probably used to this kind of food.

Mmmm, delicious!

Beside Thunderhorn, I noticed Vol muttering, "If I try one more blade of this stuff, I'm gonna lose it. I am not an **herbivore**!"

Before I knew what I was doing, I muttered to myself, "I wish I was sitting at a table laden with 𝓰𝓸𝓾𝓻𝓶𝓮𝓽 𝓬𝓱𝓮𝓮𝓼𝓮𝓼 — slices of Swiss, hunks of CHEDDAR, plates of cheesy spaghetti. . . ."

I am not an herbivore!

Hmmm . . . I wish . . .

OOPS, I ACCIDENTALLY MADE A WISH!

Suddenly, a GREEN light shot out of the medallion in my pocket, which my hand was accidentally touching. And then, a bunch of delicious food appeared in front of me!

King Skywings looked at me, **OFFENDED**. "Do you not like my banquet?" he asked.

I blushed a deep red and murmured, "Oops, I accidentally made a wish. . . ."

Oops...

Oh, how could I have been such a cheesebrain?! Now I had wasted a wish *and* made a bad impression on the King of the Unicorns.

"HOLEY CHEESE, I wish I hadn't made such a fool of myself," I whispered sadly.

Then I covered my mouth. . . .

Oops! *Oops, I did it again! I made another wish!*

This time, a **blue** light flashed, and all of the food in front of me vanished. I looked at the king and he smiled. He had forgotten what I had done. That was the good news. The bad news was the medallion had obeyed me twice, and I had wasted two wishes!

Now five of the stones were **gray**. I only had two wishes left. I made a mental note to use them only if we were in a **scary**, dangerous situation. Although I have to say eating that unicorn food was pretty **SCARY**. I don't think I'll ever look at hay the same way again!

After a wonderful night's sleep in the **blue** bedroom (the color was so calming),

I was ready to leave the next morning.

I met everyone in the gardens. We decided that King Skywings and the Unicorns of the **ROYAL GUARD** would fly us to the Land of the Diggerts. That way, we would avoid any dangers on the ground, like earthquakes, landslides, or Giant Fire-Breathing Bunny Rabbits. (Hey, you never know.)

Only Captain Coldheart would not be coming with us. He needed to return to his ship.

I thanked the captain for his help. Then I remembered something. "What will you tell your crew?" I asked him. "If they find out you helped us, they will realize you are not really **coldhearted**."

The captain **laughed**. "Don't worry, Knight. I am two steps ahead of you. I

will tell them I exchanged you prisoners for these special unicorn **potions**." He showed me a small chest filled with colored VIALS.

King Skywings added, "I gave the captain a vial from the fountain of *beauty*. Now, if one of his monsters gets tired of being a MONSTER, he can change."

After the pirate left, I climbed onto King

Skywings's back. I wanted to warn him that I wasn't the best rider, but I never got a chance.

A second later, the unicorns started to gallop. Then they spread their great **blue** wings.

The next thing I knew, we were **soaring** through the clouds. At first, I clung to the king's back for dear life. But after a while, I began to relax. It was so **Beautiful** up in the sky,

and the unicorn's back was SOFT and comfy.

We flew through the clouds for three days and three nights.

On the fourth day, we reached an area rough with sharp, ROCKY mountains.

With an elegant maneuver, the squad of unicorns landed in perfect formation at the foothills of the tallest mountain. King Skywings pointed to the entrance to a cave. "Here we are — this is the entrance to the Kingdom of the Diggerts," he announced.

As the unicorns waved good-bye, King Skywings called out to us.

"GOOD LUCK!"

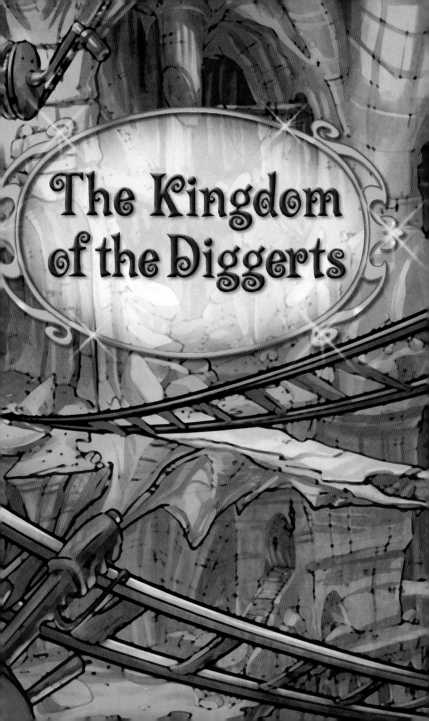

The Kingdom of the Diggerts

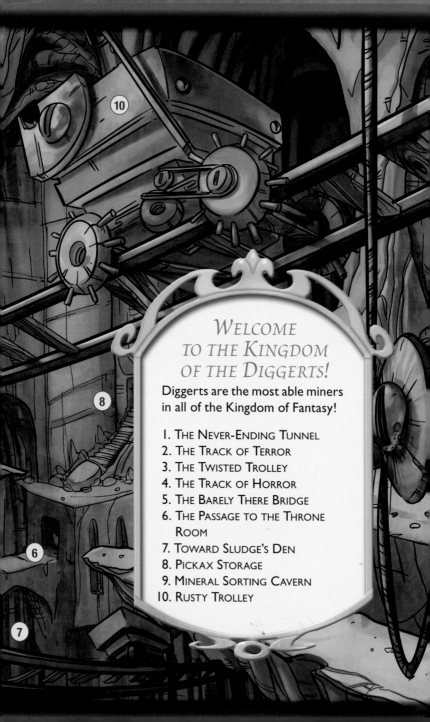

WELCOME TO THE KINGDOM OF THE DIGGERTS!

Diggerts are the most able miners in all of the Kingdom of Fantasy!

ENTER IF YOU DARE!

The first thing that I noticed was that there were no guards at the entrance to the **Kingdom of the Diggers**. How strange! King Skywings had told us on the ride over that the **Diggers** were known to be wary of outsiders. Why would they let anyone walk right in?

Thunderhorn must have sensed the same thing, because he signaled to us to stop. "Something is not right here. It could be a trap," he warned. "I will lead the way."

After just a few steps, we were immersed in **DARKNESS**. I had no idea where we were. I couldn't see a thing. It was darker than the time all the **lights** went out in my cousin Brokerat's basement apartment!

As we walked, we heard strange **metallic**

sounds around us, like hammers hitting rocks. We also heard what sounded like whispering. Was it the **WIND**, or were we being watched by **SPiES**? We advanced blindly, but suddenly Sterling **tripped** on a stone, Thunderhorn **hit** his head, Vol got **STUCK**, and I **slid** on the slippery ground and bruised my snout on an enormous rock!

Then I realized something was written on the rock in the Fantasian alphabet:

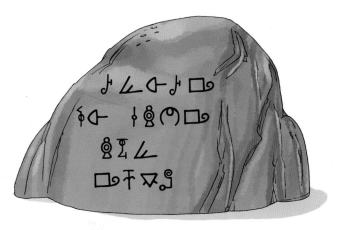

Can you translate it?*

* *You can find the Fantasian alphabet on page 310.*

It was so **DARK**, I had to trace the inscription with my pawnail to decipher it. When I did, I **gulped**.

"Ahem, it says here '*enter at your own risk*'!" I translated. "Maybe it's better if we don't go any farther."

I was hoping someone would agree with me, but to my surprise, Vol immediately began to jump **up** and **down**, clapping his hands.

"This is perfect! A real live **adventure**!" he squealed. "Maybe someone is waiting to ambush us, or maybe we will meet gigantic insects!"

"Or maybe we'll fall through a trapdoor and be imprisoned here forever," Sterling said.

"Or maybe we will all trip and land in a **HOT** underground mud spring," Thunderhorn added.

I **shivered**. Though I must admit that the last possibility didn't sound so awful. I'd read that hot mud made your fur extra-**shiny**.

I was still thinking about **shiny** fur when Thunderhorn turned. "There's only one way to find out what will happen next," he said. "We keep going!"

What could I say? Even though I was scared squeakless, Thunderhorn was right. We had to rescue **SPROUTNESS**!

But first, we needed to be able to see where we were going. So even though we only had two more wishes left, I used the **MEDALLION** to wish for some *LIGHT*.

Oooh!

Aaah!

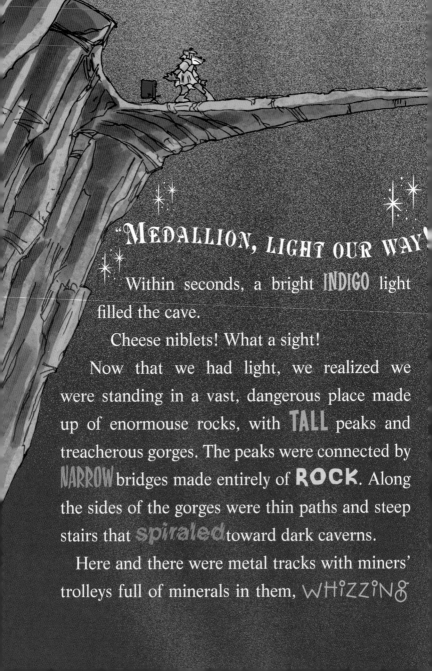

"MEDALLION, LIGHT OUR WAY!"

Within seconds, a bright INDIGO light filled the cave.

Cheese niblets! What a sight!

Now that we had light, we realized we were standing in a vast, dangerous place made up of enormouse rocks, with TALL peaks and treacherous gorges. The peaks were connected by NARROW bridges made entirely of ROCK. Along the sides of the gorges were thin paths and steep stairs that spiraled toward dark caverns.

Here and there were metal tracks with miners' trolleys full of minerals in them, WHIZZING

by. So that's what was making those scary noises.

At first, I felt relieved. Trolley cars weren't scary. Then I had another thought. No one was driving them. Could they be **HAUNTED**?

I was starting to worry when Sterling said, "Knight, we need to cross that bridge."

Now I was in a full-out panic. The bridge was as THIN as my whisker! As I stared worriedly at it, Thunderhorn grabbed Sterling's hand. "May I help you across?" he asked.

I waited for her to brush him off, but instead she accepted his help with a smile.

How strange!

ONE WRONG MOVE . . .

I had no idea what had come over Thunderhorn and Sterling. But after I took three pawsteps out onto the RAZOR-THIN bridge, I knew exactly what had come over *me*. Complete and total **fear for my life**!

One wrong move, and I was a dead rat!

Immediately, I broke out in a **sweat**...

... then my whiskers began to **tremble**!

My knees **knocked** ...

and my head began to **spin**....

Finally, I couldn't take it anymore. Did I

I can't do it!

tell you I'm deathly afraid of heights?

"I CAN'T DO IT!" I shrieked. "I can't take one more step!"

Then I lay down on the bridge. Hugging it with all four paws, I began to sob uncontrollably.

My friends tried to talk me across, but I was so far gone I barely heard a word they said.

"*I can't do it! I can't do it!*" I whimpered. *Rat-munching rattlesnakes! It can't possibly get any worse than this!* I thought.

And then it did. Right at that moment, I heard a **rumble**, and the ground began to shake.

It was the strongest **earthquake** I had ever felt!

The bridge immediately began to quiver. Sterling yelled, "Hurry, run! The bridge is about to collapse!"

Suddenly, walking across a bridge didn't

seem like such a big deal anymore. Especially now that humongous rocks and boulders were CRASHING down around me and the bridge was CRUMBLING beneath my paws. I took off like a shot!

Thunderhorn and Sterling reached the other side first and **SCREAMED** for me to hurry.

I grabbed Vol from my bag and FLUNG him to the other side of the gorge, where Thunderhorn caught him. Then I jumped, too, but I missed.

HOLEY CHEESE! I grabbed the rocky wall and was left dangling in midair!

The earth continued to shake around me, ROCKS tumbling into the chasm beneath me. I couldn't hold on for much longer. A few more

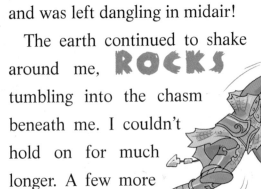

Go, hurry!

seconds, and it would all be . . . *over*!

"Good-bye, world!" I sobbed. "Tell my family I love —"

Before I could go on, I got hit in the head with a golden rope. **CLUNK!** "Great," I muttered. As if rocks weren't enough, now someone was throwing ropes at me!

Then I realized it wasn't a rope at all. It was Sterling's *golden* braid!

"Hurry, Knight! Grab on to my braid so we can pull you up!" the princess instructed.

I grabbed on to the braid with both my paws. Who would believe hair could be so strong? I mean, I'd heard about **shampoos** that were supposed to make your hair stronger, but these locks were unbreakable!

I did my best not to look down as Sterling and Thunderhorn began to hoist me up.

Meanwhile, Vol was jotting down notes.

Come on, Knight!

Help!

"This is **INCREDIBLE**! Thanks for the exciting adventure scene, Knight!" the talking book yelled. Then, when I had almost reached the top, he asked, "Do you think you could **HANG** on with one paw? You know, just dangle there for a sec? That would make this a real thriller!"

I ignored him. As if I wasn't already in enough danger! **FINALLY**, I reached the top.

I was so happy I fainted!

When I came to, Vol was fanning me with his pages.

"It's okay, Sir Geronimo. It's all over," he said.

"Am I dead?" I **croaked**.

GERONIMO
STILTON

"No," Thunderhorn answered with a chuckle. "You fainted. And nothing is over. Our ADVENTURE has just started!"

I almost cried. How much ADVENTURE could one mouse take?!

Of course, Thunderhorn was right. Our journey through the Kingdom of the Diggerts had just begun. After all, we had just arrived.

I took a deep breath to calm my nerves, then held the medallion up high to LIGHT our way. I took a few pawsteps. *See, this isn't so bad*, I told myself. I took a few more steps, bravely leading the group forward. *You can do this!* I cheered myself on. *You can —*

Suddenly, the path NARROWED, the earth gave way under my paws, and I began careening down a muddy stone slide. . . .

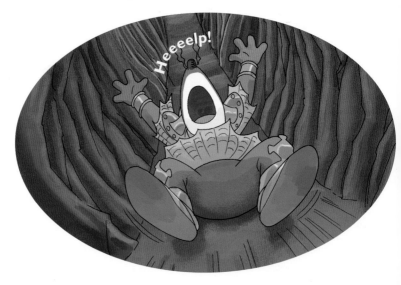

I hit the ground with a *thud*, landing in a **muddy** puddle. A second later, my friends fell on top of me.

How Gross!

We were at the bottom of some kind of pit that had really **smooth** walls.

I lifted up the medallion to shed some light and saw that we had landed in what looked like an enormouse pile of stinky garbage. There were old pickaxes, metal cans, apple cores, banana peels, and more. How **gross**!

As we felt the walls in search of something we could climb on, I suddenly heard a **CLICK**, then a *buzz*, and then the ceiling began to lower down on top of us!

Rancid rat hairs! It looked like we were about to be **CRUSHED**, ground up, and possibly **recycled** along with all of the other trash in the garbage dump!

Right then, Vol grabbed my neck and began

Help! I don't want to be ground up!

strangling me. Well, okay, he wasn't really **strangling** me, but he was holding on so tight I could barely breathe!

"Save me!" he shrieked. "I don't want to be ground up, **mashed** into pulp, and turned into toilet paper!"

"Okay, I'm thinking," I choked. Still, it was a little hard to think when your air supply was being cut off.

Just when we thought that we were going to be CRUSHED like pancakes, I suddenly heard another loud CLICK.

The ceiling stopped lowering and, slowly, it returned to its place.

We stood up, shaking off the **stinky** mud. Then we all hugged each other.

Hooray! We made it!

We made it!

Hooray!

Hooray!

Vol was so thrilled he began taking notes. "This is unbelievable! What an adventure! I've got to get this down!" he gushed.

But a minute later, he stopped as we all listened to a strange noise coming from somewhere above us. It was kind of a gurgling rumble. . . .

What could it have been?

We didn't have to wait too long to find out. Within seconds, a door opened above us, and an endless stream of WATER poured down on top of us!

The water level started to RISE . . . RISE . . . RISE . . . RISE . . .

Oh, what a way to go! Just when I thought I would drown like a sewer rat, I heard another CLICK, and the floor opened up beneath us. Where were we headed? Down the drain!

1) WE ENDE
   UP IN TH
   DIGGERT
   ENORMOU
   GARBAGE
   DUMP!
   BLECH!

2) THE CEILING
   BEGAN TO
   LOWER:
   WE WERE
   ABOUT
   TO BE
   CRUSHED!
   WHAT A
   FRIGHT!

3) THEN A GIGANTIC STREAM OF WATER RAINED DOWN ON US FROM ABOVE! WHAT AN ADVENTURE!

WE WERE ABOUT TO BE TOTALLY SUBMERGED WHEN THE BOTTOM OF OUR PRISON OPENED UP LIKE A DRAIN AND WE ENDED UP DOWN THE SEWER!

A THOUSAND LITTLE GREEN MONSTERS

I was doing my best to stay afloat when Vol climbed onto my head.

"My ink is **running**!" he cried, flipping his pages frantically. "Maybe you can read something about the **sewer system**, Knight, and we can figure out what to do."

He stuck a page in front of me and I read it:

SEWER:
a series of underground canals gathering wastewaters that come from sink drains, showers, toilets, and other places . . .

"We could swim against the CURRENT and then find our way out through another drain," I suggested.

Of course, swimming against the CURRENT was easier said than done. Did I mention I'm not really a sportsmouse?

As I was slogging along, I noticed a swarm of little yellow eyes blinking at us in the dark. My whiskers shook with fear.

I held the medallion up so we could get a

better look and gasped. The YELLOW eyes belonged to a swarm of little GREEN monsters covered in scales! They looked like giant lizards in uniform.

As the creatures surrounded us, Thunderhorn drew his **SWORD**, Sterling lifted her bow, and I tried to hold the light steady. It wasn't easy. I was shaking like a leaf!

"Sorry, I can't help," Vol apologized. "But I can't get my paper wet!"

The monsters **GNASHED** their teeth.

"Paper! Did that guy say he was made of paper?! We love paper! Attack!" they cried.

I would have fainted, but Vol beat me to it.

"Run, Knight, bring the book to safety!" Sterling yelled. Then she turned to face the monsters.

Ooof!

Vol, you're so heavy!

"How dare you pick on a little **ENCYCLOPEDIA**!" she scolded.

As I fled, Thunderhorn stayed behind to help the princess.

I spotted a metal ladder and climbed up it, clutching Vol by my side. Moldy mozzarella, was the ladder slippery!

Just when I was ready to give up, I saw a grate over my head. Slowly, I pushed it aside.

I found myself in a strange bathroom with walls carved out of dark **granite**. The sink had a gray marble countertop and solid **GOLD** faucets. The mirror was made of rock crystal and there was an inscription above it that read: "The Royal Bathroom of the King T.T."

At that moment, I heard some voices coming from outside. I opened the door and peeked out.

I saw a room lit by FLAMING torches. It was packed with Diggerts. They were listening intently to one Diggert, who appeared to be their king. He was wearing a dark robe and gold crown and sat on an enormouse **THRONE**.

As I watched, I noticed something odd. All of the Diggerts, even the king, seemed to be **DOWN**

THE ROYAL BATHROOM OF THE KING T.T.

IN THE DUMPS. I wondered why. Captain Coldheart had said that the Diggerts were the happiest when they were working. He even said they liked to **sing**. The only kinds of songs I could see this group singing were the **BLUES**!

"Your Majesty, you must do something!" one of the Diggerts pleaded, stepping forward.

The king sighed. "My dear subjects, I'm afraid there is nothing I can do. **SLUDGE** has imprisoned the women and children, even my beloved wife, Eartha. I cannot put them in danger. We must keep digging for **STINKSTONE**. It's what he wants," he said.

The crowd groaned. "But, Your **Majesty**, he will never leave. He knows he can only get **STINKSTONE** from our mines. We'll be digging forever!" another **Diggert** wailed. "And after he kidnapped that maiden, the **earthquakes** started up. The tunnels are even more **DANGEROUS**!"

I jumped. I had no idea what stinkstone was or who Sludge was, but could the maiden be **SPROUTNESS**?

I leaned against the door to hear better, but right then Vol woke up, grabbed my neck, and shrieked, "**Knight!**"

The door burst open, and I *rolled* forward into the throne room. Vol and I were captured and tied up along with two other prisoners . . . Thunderhorn and Sterling!

Who are you and what are you doing here?

KING T.T.

"Who are you dirty **rotten** scoundrels and what are you doing here?" demanded the king.

Thunderhorn spoke first. "I am **THUNDERHORN**, King of the Elves!" he proclaimed. "And I have never been so insulted! Order your men to untie us immediately!"

Then Sterling said, "I am Sterling, the Princess of the Silver Dragons, and I have never been so humiliated!"

Finally, Vol piped up. "I am **FIRST VOLUME**, a talking book from the Great Explanatorium, and . . . I am so upset, I am left without words!"

The King of the Diggerts turned **RED** in embarrassment. "Oops, sorry! You didn't look like noble mice . . . I mean books . . . I mean creatures . . . what I'm trying to say is, I am KING

KING TYLER TERRAIN III

Tyler Terrain III, the Daring Lord of the Rocky Tunnels, Defender of the Muddy Miners, and Keeper of the Caves, rules over his people, the Diggerts, together with his wife, the noble Eartha of the Clays, descendant of Boulderella the Beautiful and Crystal the Kind.

King Terrain is called the Daring because he defended his kingdom during the famous invasion of the giant earthworms. He is also known for being the composer of some of the most famous songs of the Diggerts. They are so beautiful they can soften even the hardest of stones.

TYLER TERRAIN III, the Daring Lord of the Rocky Tunnels, Defender of the Muddy Miners, and Keeper of the Caves. But you can call me King T. T., if you want."

It was then that I realized we still smelled like the stinky sewer. Yuck! No wonder the king thought we were dirty rotten scoundrels! Maybe if I explained things, he would let us take baths in the royal bathroom. Maybe he even had a rubber

Sigh!

Your Majesty, help us!

ducky I could borrow, like the one I had at home (not that anyone needed to know about it).

I shook my head. FOCUS, I told myself. Then I explained to the king that we were looking for Sproutness and trying to figure out what was causing the earthquakes.

King T.T. shook his head sadly. "About a week ago, Sludge's little monsters **kidnapped** a young maiden. I suppose it could be Sproutness," he said with a sigh. "But I'm afraid I can't help you, Knight. **Sludge** is keeping all of the women and children, including my wife, hostage."

I tried getting the king to explain who Sludge was, but he didn't seem to hear me and kept on talking.

"You see, Sludge is obsessed with STINKSTONE," he went on. "He can't get enough of it. My subjects have been working night and day in the STINKSTONE mines, and they're worn out. But what am I going to do? If we stop **MINING**, who knows what Sludge will do to our families?"

At that moment, something **SNAPPED** inside me — I felt myself growing angry. Who did this Sludge guy think he was, anyway? He seemed like nothing but a big **BULLY**.

"**Somebody** needs to stop Sludge!" I squeaked, stepping forward.

"We'll help you, Knight!" Thunderhorn and Sterling offered.

"Me, too!" Vol added.

I gulped. When I said "somebody," I didn't mean **ME**! But it was too late. Sterling and Thunderhorn **clapped** me on the back, and Vol **hugged** me. Then they all

shouted, "**We can do it!**"

I couldn't believe I had volunteered to take on an **evil** villain with a name like **Sludge**. But there was no turning back — everyone was counting on me. My friends **SMILED** broadly at me. Actually, I think Thunderhorn and Sterling were smiling at each other. In fact, something told me those two were becoming the best of *friends*!

After my friends were done promising to **Stick** by my side, they grew quiet, waiting for my plan of action.

"**Ahem**, well, yes," I stammered, trying to appear **BRAVE** and in charge of the situation. "I think we need to start with this **Sludge** guy. So, um, King T.T., can

FRIENDSHIP

Friendship is one of the most precious things there is. Good friends lift us up when we are feeling down and celebrate our successes with us. Friends may give advice, but they do not judge us. Friends accept us for who we are and do not try to change us. If we are lucky, we will have many good friends in our lives.

you tell us who **SLUDGE** is?"

At this, my friends turned to me in shock and cried, "You don't know who **SLUDGE** is?!"

So much for feeling in charge of the situation.

King T.T. put his hand on my shoulder. "Knight, imagine someone — or should I say some*thing* — **evil**, awful, scary, monstrous, intimidating, unpredictable, unbelievable. Well, that's **SLUDGE**, the Monster of a Thousand Faces," he explained.

I turned as pale as a slice of mozzarella.

"But wait, I have an idea," the king went on. "If you **DRESS UP** like Diggerts, you can work in the stinkstone mines and investigate without getting caught."

Then he clapped his hands, and two Diggerts with long **BRAIDED** beards and **MUSCULAR** arms arrived.

"Meet **GRAVEL** and **MULCH**, my trusty advisors!" he said, introducing them.

He ordered them to turn us into perfect Diggerts by the next morning.

"Can you make this happen?" he asked them.

Gravel and Mulch nodded their mighty heads. "You can count on us, Your Majesty!" they bellowed in deep, BOOMING voices.

Then they took us to another room, and there our transformation began . . .

After hours and hours of TREATMENT, we really looked like Diggerts!

Unfortunately, however, Gravel and Mulch were not satisfied. They said that we needed to

GRAVEL

MULCH

HERE IS HOW THEY TURNED US INTO DIGGERTS

1 First, to make us look like Diggerts, we spread a thick layer of sticky clay over ourselves.

2 Then we got our hands — and paws! — and nails dirty by digging in the dirt.

3 They made us put on Diggert clothing: earth-colored tunics, earth-colored pants, and earth-colored cloaks.

4 Then we disguised ourselves with long braided beards and gave ourselves new names. . . .

CLAY

QUARTZY

GRANITH

ROCKER

learn how to use **pickaxes** like skilled miners.

So they made us train for about seven hundred hours (or something like that) breaking rocks with enormouse pickaxes. Oh, my poor *aching* back! I made a mental note to call Dr. Crackinback, my chiropractor, when I got home.

Then, just when I thought things couldn't get any worse, Gravel and Mulch told us we needed to get used to the **scent** of stinkstone. So they locked us in a **dark** cave filled with the strange mineral.

Vol **RUFFLED** his pages to get some air, Thunderhorn plugged his nose, and Sterling tied a piece of her clothing around her face.

As for me . . . well, I just fainted!

The stench was awful!

SLUDGE, THE MONSTER OF A THOUSAND FACES

The next morning, we started to work in the mines just like real Diggerts. It was exhausting work. And the stench was sickening!

When the day was over, we dragged ourselves to the dormitory caves with **aching** backs and lots of BLISTERS.

That night, the four of us sat around a limestone

I'm exhausted!

Ow, ow!

table in the cafeteria with the other Diggerts and ate bowls of SOUP that tasted like mud. Ugh! How could the Diggerts eat this slop? I thought about asking someone if there was a PIZZA PLACE nearby, but something told me they wouldn't deliver.

As we ate, we began to talk among ourselves. I was so worried about Sludge.

"What does Sludge LOOK like?" I asked my friends.

But before they could answer, one of the Diggerts spoke up. "He's a giant spider that drools a stinky and **poisonous** liquid. . . ." he began.

"You're wrong. He has crab claws and a rhinoceros horn," another Diggert interrupted.

Then they all began to talk at once.

"What are you talking about? He has octopus tentacles and razor-sharp teeth. . . ."

"No, he is pale, almost transparent, wears a **BLACK** cape, and has deep **RED** eyes like fire."

At that point, my head was spinning like a top. What were these Diggerts talking about? Why did everyone have a different description of the same creature?!

I was still trying to figure it all out when Vol tapped me on the paw. "Knight . . . I mean . . . Quartzy, I found a chapter on famous MONSTERS. Read it, it's interesting. . . ."

The ancient Greeks believed in the existence of extraordinary monsters like Cerberus, the dog with three heads; harpies, who are part-woman, part-bird; and Scylla and Charybdis, who are sea monsters.

It is said that in the Kingdom of Diggerts there lives a creature named Sludge, Monster of a Thousand Faces. He lives in the deepest gorges, feeds on fear, and takes on the appearance of his victims' greatest fears.

As soon as I finished reading, I got an idea.

"I may have discovered Sludge's **secret**," I whispered to the others. "It sounds like he takes the shape of everyone's worst **fears**. Each one of us has different **fears**, which is why Sludge looks different to everyone."

"So if someone had no fears, what **shape** would Sludge take?" Vol asked, perplexed.

I told Vol that's what we needed to find out. But first we had to track down Sludge.

"Great idea, Knight," the talking book agreed. "Let's go! I don't want to miss out on any of this **ADVENTURE**! This is going to be great!"

"I'm in," agreed Sterling.

"Me, too," said Thunderhorn. "But we need to be careful. We don't want Sludge to know we are looking for him. We should **surprise** him."

We waited until all of the Diggerts in the cave had fallen asleep. How did we know they were

sleeping? They were snoring so loudly, I could hardly think straight!

We crept away into the dark, through tunnels and over narrow bridges. I had no idea where we were. The place was a maze! My heart was pounding and my whiskers were shaking with fear!

"Get a grip," I told myself. I could only discover Sludge's real self if I had no fear. I tried to think of every way I could to be more courageous.

THE SECRETS TO BEING MORE COURAGEOUS

- Courage is not an instinct, but a virtue that you can cultivate.
- Only by facing your fears can you overcome them.
- Try to remain calm when you feel yourself becoming scared. Getting upset will only make things worse.
- If you are scared, breathe deeply, because when you breathe out, you release tension.
- The more you test yourself, the more you gain courage and confidence. Facing your fears more and more often will make you gain trust in yourself.
- Never face dangerous situations just to be admired. Being courageous does not mean being reckless!

As we walked, I tried to practice my courage-building techniques. "Remain calm," I chanted over and over. Then I took some deep breaths. But as we got closer to the bottom of the gorge, the smell of STINKSTONE grew stronger, and I ended up having a coughing fit.

Rats! What if Sludge heard me? So much for courage-building. Now I was even more NERVOUS than before. Oh, how did I get myself into these messes?

Just then, we heard some noises coming from the other side of the rock wall. A minute later, a deep voice thundered, "When will that STINKSTONE prison be done for Sproutness, the Fairy of the Earth? I don't have all YEAR, you know! I'm a very busy **monster**! Sproutness is already very weak from the smell of the STINKSTONE, but if she's locked in a prison made entirely of STINKSTONE, she'll be even weaker. Then I, Sludge, the Monster of a Thousand Faces, can steal all her power and take over the entire Kingdom of Fantasy!"

A smaller voice responded, "Yes, Your Monsterness. The Diggerts are working double shifts to finish it, Your Monsterness, and —"

Sludge interrupted in a SINGSONG voice, *"Yes, Your Monsterness. They're working, Your Monsterness.* Enough with the chatter. Just do it!"

Suddenly, I noticed a crack in the wall above us. Sterling climbed onto Thunderhorn's shoulders, Vol climbed onto Sterling's shoulders, and I climbed onto Vol. I peeked through the crack and saw a dark cavern. Sproutness was imprisoned in one cage, and in another were the Diggert women and children.

What a TERRIBLE sight!

1. SLUDGE'S THRONE
2. MACHINE FOR STEALING
   SPROUTNESS'S FAIRY POWER
3. STINKSTONE CAVE
4. SLUDGE'S LITTLE MONSTERS
5. OBLIVION RIVER
6. STINKSTONE CELL, WHERE
   SPROUTNESS IS HELD PRISONER
7. THE DIGGERTS' CELL

SLUDGE'S TRUE FACE!

I got down and told my friends everything that I had seen. I felt awful. Sproutness looked as if she was fading away, and the Diggerts looked so sad. I also saw (and **smelled**!) the stinkstone and these huge cable wires connected to what looked like Sludge's throne. A smelly little river seemed to be the only entryway into the cavern.

"Now what do we do?" Vol asked, trembling.

"We need to return to the cave and convince all of the Diggerts to help us," Thunderhorn said decisively. "We can't fight Sludge and his little monsters alone. And only the Diggerts know how to reach Sludge's cave."

My friends headed down the **TUNNEL**, with Thunderhorn leading the way.

I followed them, but I guess I was *lagging* behind because I was too busy thinking about everything we had just seen in the cavern. Sproutness . . . the Diggerts . . . the strange throne and the prison cells . . . The next thing I knew I had walked right into a wall of the tunnel! **BANG!**

That's when I heard a *buzzing* noise. Then the wall of the tunnel opened up, I rolled forward, and the wall suddenly closed behind me! I was so scared that I started punching the wall and screaming, "HELP! Let me out!"

Let me out!

But no one heard me. I turned around and noticed, in HORROR, that I was now at the bottom of the dark and stinky gorge, and something was *moving* behind me.

A voice hissed at my back, "Turn around, rat, and look me in the eyes!"

IT WAS SLUDGE!

I was trembling from my tail to my whiskers, and I saw . . . an enormouse cat, with eyes as red as F𝕀ℝ𝔼 and teeth as sharp as knives, ready to devour me.

What a **fur-raising** sight! Sludge had turned into the most terrifying thing for us mice: a giant cat!

Then I remembered that Sludge feeds on fear, and I forced myself to breathe calmly. My heartbeat

slowed and I was able to think of happy things, like my friends, my family, Sproutness, the Diggerts, **chocolate cheesy chews**. . . .

Suddenly, I wasn't afraid anymore. I felt strong and confident, and even a little hungry. Oh, how I love my cheesy chews! But I'd never taste another one if I didn't do something soon, so I stood up and yelled, **"SLUDGE, I'M NOT AFRAID!"**

I looked up and stared directly into Sludge's evil **RED** eyes. It was then that I saw Sludge's true face.

It was just as I thought. Sludge didn't have a

SLUDGE'S TRUE FACE!

Sludge comes from an ancient line of mud monsters: He is the son of the great Mudward II and Glopella VI.

He was born in the darkest of dark and has always lived deep in a hole of stinky sludge. His secret dream is to become human, and that is why he wants the powers of Sproutness, the Fairy of the Earth.

Sludge appears to have a thousand faces because he takes the face of everyone's fears. Only looking at him without fear reveals his true face: a mountain of shapeless mud, with two eyes the color of fire. The only thing that Sludge fears is water, because it can melt him.

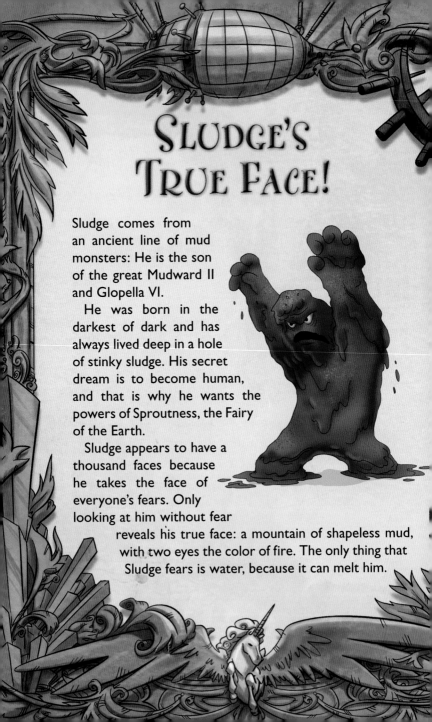

face! Instead he had two FIRE-COLORED eyes set in a mountain of **mud**.

Next thing I knew, the muddy monster grabbed me with his big gloppy hand.

"Say your good-byes, **MOUSE**!" he thundered. "I won't let you go around telling everyone what I really look like, not when I am about to take a human form thanks to the power of Sproutness! But now, look me in the eyes. . . ."

I would have replied, but as I stared at Sludge's GLOWING red eyes, I realized that I was getting **VERY, VERY, VERY SLEEPY**.

Sludge watched me and chuckled. "That's right, mouse. Look right into my eyes. You're getting tired, aren't you?"

I tried to resist, but I couldn't keep my eyelids open. Before I knew it, I'd fallen asleep.

MINE! ALL MINE!

When I woke up, I found myself with a heavy **chain** locked around my paw. I was in the stinkstone prison along with Sproutness. The **STENCH** was enough to make a grown mouse cry!

The first thing I noticed was that the prison of **STINKSTONE** had been finished. Who knows how long I had been sleeping for! Had it been days?

At that moment, Sludge opened the door to our cell. "How are my favorite prisoners today?" He chuckled cruelly. Then he turned to Sproutness. "Today's the day. Today I will transfer all your **POWER** from you to me. I will take on a human form and the **Kingdom of Fantasy** will be mine! All mine!"

Sludge linked the chains around Sproutness's wrists to the armrests of his throne. It seemed that somehow Sludge had figured out a way to harness Sproutness's magic.

"**STOP!**" I yelled. But I knew it was useless. I mean, let's face it, how do you reason with a big **blob** of mud?

"Try and stop me! You can't do anything, and neither can she!" Sludge roared. "She no longer has any strength to resist. Stinkstone **WEAKENS**

What should I do?

fairies! That's right. When I first captured her, she **shook** her chains so much we had earthquakes every day. What a pain! I'm telling you . . ."

As Sludge rambled on and on about stinkstone and fairies and earthquakes, my brain was *racing* at warp speed.

I needed to do something, and soon! But what? I still had the **medallion** with me, but how should I use it? I only had **ONE** wish left, so I only had one chance!

Should I **FREE SPROUTNESS**? But then Sludge could just capture her again. Was it better to wish for something else?

> **DIFFICULT DECISIONS**
> Sometimes we need to make difficult decisions, and we don't know what to do. Sometimes it helps if we make a list of the pros and cons that would result if we make a certain choice. If we put our thoughts down on paper, the right solution may be easier to see.

Could I use the medallion to take away Sludge's power forever? But then how would I free Sproutness, who was getting WEAKER before my eyes?

Oh, what should I do?

I was still trying to make a choice when right then a loud noise erupted from the mines.

RUMBLE RUMBLE RUMBLE!

It almost sounded like **THUNDER**.

Then, without warning, an enormouse flood of **WATER** burst into the cavern. *The River of Oblivion was overflowing!*

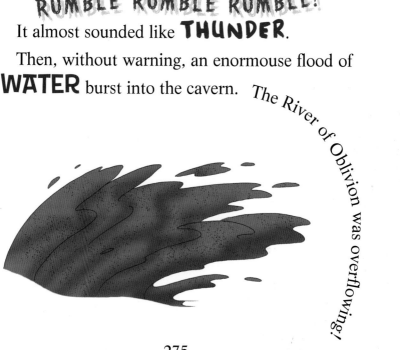

Sludge clambered away to the corner of the cavern. "No, not **WATER**!" he shrieked. "I'm afraid of water! Get my wet suit! Get my life raft! Get my mommy!"

In a flash, the water level began to **rise**. . . .

What was it with **RISING** water and this place? Were we about to be headed for another sewer drain?

I want my mommy!!

Right then I spotted Sproutness. Holey cheese! She was about to go under!

Without thinking, I grabbed the medallion and squeaked, "SAVE HER!"

A **purple** ray of light shot out of the medallion and broke Sproutness's chains. Then the ray turned into a **bubble** of light, lifted her out of the water, and brought her to safety.

As I struggled to keep afloat, I turned toward Sludge and saw that he was MELTING in the water!

After a few moments, he was just a spot of mud. Then the current from the River of Oblivion carried him away, into the depths of the deep gorge from which he had come.

I would have cheered, but I was too busy trying to not **drown**! I'm too fond of my fur!

I WAS SAVED!

Then a miracle happened. The current broke the chain that was holding me. I rose to the surface. I felt someone grip my paw and lift me out of the water. I was saved!

I coughed, **RUBBED** my eyes, and looked around. I was sitting on a raft next to Thunderhorn, Sterling, Vol, and Sproutness!

I was relieved to see that Sproutness looked a little better. A bizarre fleet of boats made out of BARRELS, planks of wood, TIRES, and lots of other things floated all around us. On top of the boats were the cheering Diggerts. They had reached Sludge's cave by floating along the River of Oblivion.

On one of the rafts stood King T.T., with a huge smile on his face.

The king cleared his throat and said, "My loyal subjects, tonight is a time to **CELEBRATE**. Sludge will never **THREATEN** us again. He has **DISAPPEARED** forever down the River of Oblivion, because he was really only a mud monster, as the Knight has shown us!"

"Hooray!" everyone cheered.

I was so relieved that everyone was safe and that I hadn't **DROWNED**, I started cheering myself.

We did it!

Hooray!

After all, what are the chances that an unathletic mouse like me would survive a near drowning **twice** in one adventure? I made a decision right then and there to make sure to sign up for a refresher swim course when I got back to Mouse Island. You can never be too **PREPARED**!

When everyone stopped cheering, King T.T. began speaking again, in a serious tone.

"My dear subjects, Sludge has been defeated, but our caverns are flooded. We cannot live here anymore," he explained.

You are welcome!

Thank you!

But Thunderhorn made the king an offer. "I would **love** for you to be guests in the Kingdom of the Elves," he began. "I will give you an entire mountain, rich with **minerals** and **precious** stones. You can build a brand-new underground kingdom, but only on **ONE CONDITION**. . . ."

The cave fell silent. Everyone waited and waited and **WAITED**.

Time passed. My fur grew longer.

Finally, I couldn't stand the **SUSPENSE**, so I asked, "What's the **condition**, Thunderhorn?"

And he replied, "The condition is that you must never mine for stinkstone! It really stinks!"

Then the King and all the Diggerts burst out laughing.

Ha, ha, ha! *Ha, ha, ha!* *Ha, ha, ha!* *Ha, ha, ha!*

We all floated down the River of Oblivion, which led us out of the mountain and into the daylight. I was so happy to see the sky again. No offense to the Diggerts, but I have to say, living **underground** just isn't for this mouse.

I was enjoying the view and the air when someone began **CHOKING** me! Had Sludge come back to haunt me?

No, it was only Vol **clutching** my neck and shouting, "I can't believe it, Knight! My dream of becoming a real adventure book is coming true! Now tell me everything that happened in the cave with Sludge. And don't leave out any **JUICY** details!"

So I told Vol the whole story about the rising river, Sludge **melting**, and using the medallion to save Sproutness.

As I was squeaking, I pulled the **medallion** out of my pocket, remembering. All of a sudden, I **remembered** something else. The medallion actually belonged to SPROUTNESS. So I gave it back to her. When the fairy put it around her neck, she immediately regained her strength.

PICTURE PERFECT!

We sailed for many long days along the winding River of Oblivion until one night we reached another river.

Thunderhorn recognized it immediately. It was the Sparkling River, which crosses through to the Kingdom of the Elves.

From there we kept paddling until we reached **SERENITY LAKE**, right in the heart of the Kingdom of the Elves.

It was so peaceful!

Serenity Lake sparkled in the **silver** light of the moon, and majestic trees lined its banks. It looked like Princess Emerald and the Elves had been hard at work repairing the **DAMAGE** the earthquakes had caused. There wasn't a blade of grass out of place. It was picture perfect!

When we reached the center of the lake, we heard the MUSIC of silver flutes and suddenly a thousand TORCHES lit up the calm waters.

Everyone cheered as our raft approached. I saw many of my new and old friends from the Kingdom of Fantasy. I guess word had gotten out about our **success** on our mission. You know, defeating Sludge, freeing Sproutness, helping the Diggerts, and all the rest.

"**Surprise!**" Em shouted, waving her arms in the air.

"Surprise! Surprise!" the crowd roared.

At first I felt a little shy. I mean, I'm not big on surprise parties. One time my cousin Trap threw me a surprise party at my house and I was still wearing my **pajamas**! But when I looked around at all of the smiling faces, I had to **smile**. It felt good to be appreciated.

After we landed, Em summoned an elf who

arrived with a GOLDEN key on a red velvet pillow.

She gave it to King Thunderhorn with a little bow.

"Here you go, brother," she said. "The KEY to your kingdom. We worked together to plant trees, fill the RIFTS, and dry the flooded land. Sorry I gave you a hard time about sending me back. I understand why you did it. The elves needed me, and I'm glad we got things back to normal."

Thunderhorn took the key with a smile. Then he announced for all to hear, "Princess Emerald, you

The key to your kingdom!

Thanks, Em!

have governed with **kindness** and wisdom! From now on we will lead the kingdom together, side by side!"

Then Thunderhorn turned to me, handing me the golden **KEY** to the kingdom. "And I would like to give this key to a special rodent who has run to our aid and faced a thousand dangers to help us. Sir Geronimo of Stilton, our kingdom will always be open to you!" he declared.

I accepted the giant key with a grin, shoving it into my pocket and accidentally poking myself with it. **YOUCH!** How embarrassing!

For you!

Thank you!

Then Princess Em said, "Let the **PARTY** begin!"

Everyone began talking at once. I saw Professor Longwind chatting happily with Thunderhorn. I was glad to see they had made **PEACE** with each other.

I saw all the scientists and scholars from the Great Explanatorium, and **VOL** had reunited with eleven of his brothers from the Talking Library.

Captain Coldheart was there with his crew of monsters, who set off lightning and

Scholars from the Explanatorium

First Volume

Professor Longwind

Captain Coldheart and his crew

thunder in our honor. And KING SKYWINGS was there with his court.

I also saw Cozy and Factual, the King and Queen of the Gnomes, along with my dear friend Scribblehopper. Nearby were Blossom, the **Queen of the Fairies**, and her husband, George, the King of Dreams.

I was amazed at how many friends had come out to celebrate our victory. There was only one friend who I hadn't seen, and that

Blossom and George

King Skywings

Cozy and Factual

Scribblehopper

was the **DRAGON OF THE RAINBOW**. Where could he be? I decided to take a look around for him, and so I slipped away from the crowd and took a little stroll around the elfin land.

It really was a **MAGICAL** place. I ambled through soft green grass, past babbling brooks and flowering trees. Eventually, I came to a place called Lover's Spring. And that's when I saw them.

There, under the first rays of the **SUNLIGHT**, were Thunderhorn and Sterling. The King of the Elves had taken Sterling's hand and was kneeling before her. "My sweet Sterling, I love you! Will you marry me?" he asked. And she replied, "**YES!**"

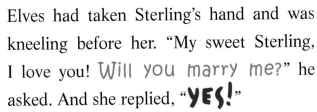

I was so embarrassed at having eavesdropped on such a special moment that I turned to sneak off — but I tripped and fell right into the water. **SPLASH!**

Luckily, Thunderhorn and Sterling only had **EYES** for each other. But when I got back to the party I told Vol, and he said he wasn't surprised.

"You want to know when they fell in **love**, Knight?" he asked.

He showed me a picture of the **Fountain of Love** in the Kingdom of the Blue Unicorns. Only then did I remember that Thunderhorn

and Sterling had fallen in the fountain when they were **dueling**!

I scratched my head. "So does that mean they **love** each other only because they fell in the fountain?" I asked Vol.

The book just shook his head wisely. "Not exactly, Knight," he said. "They love each other because every true love is already **WRITTEN** in the stars. Sometimes all you need is a bit of encouragement so that the love can blossom."

A few minutes later, the two **LOVEBIRDS** returned and announced their big news. Everyone applauded for them and yelled, "Congratulations!" Blossom, Sproutness, and Em cried tears of joy. And me?

Well, I was just about to wish them well when a voice **sang** over my shoulder, "Hello, Knight!"

It was the Dragon of the **RAINBOW**!

I was so excited, I climbed on his back. To

CELEBRATE, he began a series of acrobatic tricks. I immediately lost my balance and began to fall and fall and fall and fall and fall and fall and fall and fall and fall and fall and fall and fall and fall and fall and fall and fall for what seemed like eternity. . . .

Until I hit my head on something hard and *fainted*.

The Return
Home . . .

WELCOME TO MOUSE ISLAND!

Mouse Island is the place where every mouse would love to live!

I'll Get Him Up!

Suddenly, I heard someone yelling, "Make room, make room, make ROOOOOM, let me handle my cousin! I'll get him up!"

And the next thing I knew, I was hit with a bucketful of **freezing** water!

At that point, my eyes opened, and I saw a chubby snout and a familiar Hawaiian shirt.

SPLAAAASH!

It was TRAP! Behind him was my nephew BENJAMIN.

"You see? I was right! He just needed some shock therapy! Nothing like a bucket of ICE WATER to the snout to wake someone up," Trap insisted. "Right, Cuz? You can thank me anytime. I accept cash, lottery tickets, *SPORTS CARS* . . ."

I sat up, wiping my fur. "What am I doing here?" I mumbled.

I was right!

Huh?

I felt as if I'd been away for days and days.

Trap snorted. "Germeister, the problem is that you faint so easily! One little clunk to the old noggin, and you fall into the land of dreams. I think you do it on purpose so you can take a little NAP. . . ." he said.

At that point, Benjamin hugged me, looking worried. "Uncle, don't you remember?" he squeaked. "We were climbing **MARBLEHEAD MOUNTAIN**, you stuffed yourself on energy bars, then you went to go get some water and fell down!"

Just then, it all came rushing back to me. That mysterious letter, that mysterious appointment at noon. Oh, no! Was I late for the

APPOINTMENT?

"We have to go!" I cried.

With **incredible**

For Geronimo Stilton

PERSONAL

EXTREMELY URGENT

effort, and with Benjamin's help, I stood up. Everything **hurt**, every little bit of me, from the top of my ears to the end of my tail.

Well, okay, maybe I'm **EXAGGERATING** a bit. There was one whisker (the third from the left on my right side) that was okay. But the rest of me was a wreck!

Benjamin grabbed my paw. "Don't worry, Uncle," he soothed. "We'll help you. It's just a few more feet to the top of **MARBLEHEAD MOUNTAIN**."

So, with difficulty, I headed toward the top. And when I got there, my mouth fell open in shock.

There were all of my friends, yelling, "Surprise!"

SURPRISE!!! SURPRISE!!! SURPRISE!!! SURPRISE!!! SURPRISE!!!

They had organized a **SURPRISE** party for me!

I couldn't have been any more surprised!

Waiting at the top of the mountain were my friends, my relatives, and all of the staffers from *The Rodent's Gazette*.

They had organized a wonderful picnic with **CAKES**, pies, **SANDWICHES**, and lots of other treats. There was even a humongous strawberry cheesecake.

And, of course, the best part of all was that at **THIS** surprise party, I wasn't wearing my **PAJAMAS**!

Soon everyone was singing:

HAPPY BIRTHDAY TO YOU,
HAPPY BIRTHDAY,
DEAR GERONIMO!

I thanked everyone. I had forgotten all about my birthday.

Then Thea and Petunia Pretty Paws gave me a RED velvet pillow with a golden key on it. "On behalf of everyone, we want you to have this key to our hearts," they said.

I was touched. As I always say, friends and family are the greatest gift of all!

But, to tell you the truth, it seemed as if I had seen that key somewhere before . . . maybe in a dream . . . or maybe in the **Kingdom of Fantasy**!

ABOUT THE AUTHOR

Born in New Mouse City, Mouse Island, **GERONIMO STILTON** is Rattus Emeritus of Mousomorphic Literature and of Neo-Ratonic Comparative Philosophy. For the past twenty years, he has been running *The Rodent's Gazette*, New Mouse City's most widely read daily newspaper.

Stilton was awarded the Ratitzer Prize for his scoops on *The Curse of the Cheese Pyramid* and *The Search for Sunken Treasure*. He has also received the Andersen 2000 Prize for Personality of the Year. One of his bestsellers won the 2002 eBook Award for world's best ratlings' electronic book. His works have been published all over the globe.

In his spare time, Mr. Stilton collects antique cheese rinds and plays golf. But what he most enjoys is telling stories to his nephew Benjamin.

THE KINGDOM OF FANTASY

THE QUEST FOR PARADISE:
THE RETURN TO THE KINGDOM OF FANTASY

THE AMAZING VOYAGE:
THE THIRD ADVENTURE IN THE KINGDOM OF FANTASY

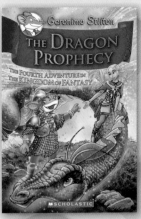

THE DRAGON PROPHECY:
THE FOURTH ADVENTURE IN THE KINGDOM OF FANTASY

Check out these very special editions featuring me and the Thea Sisters!

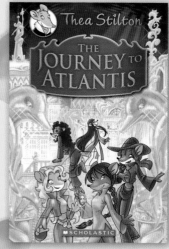

THE JOURNEY TO ATLANTIS

THE SECRET OF THE FAIRIES

Don't miss any of my other fabumouse adventures!

#1 Lost Treasure of the Emerald Eye

#2 The Curse of the Cheese Pyramid

#3 Cat and Mouse in a Haunted Hou

#4 I'm Too Fond of My Fur!

#5 Four Mice Deep in the Jungle

#6 Paws Off, Cheddarface!

#7 Red Pizzas for a Blue Count

#8 Attack of Bandit Cats

#9 A Fabumouse Vacation for Geronimo

#10 All Because of a Cup of Coffee

#11 It's Halloween, You 'Fraidy Mouse!

#12 Merry Christmas, Geronimo!

#13 The Phant of the Subwa

#14 The Temple of the Ruby of Fire

#15 The Mona Mousa Code

#16 A Cheese-Colored Camper

#17 Watch Your Whiskers, Stilton!

#18 Shipwreck the Pirate Isla

#19 My Name Is Stilton, Geronimo Stilton

#20 Surf's Up, Geronimo!

#21 The Wild, Wild West

#22 The Secret of Cacklefur Castle

A Christmas Tale

#23 Valentine's Day Disaster

#24 Field Trip to Niagara Falls

#25 The Search for Sunken Treasure

#26 The Mummy with No Name

#27 The Christmas Toy Factory

#28 Wedding Crasher

#29 Down and Out Down Under

#30 The Mouse Island Marathon

#31 The Mysterious Cheese Thief

Christmas Catastrophe

#32 Valley of the Giant Skeletons

#33 Geronimo and the Gold Medal Mystery

#34 Geronimo Stilton, Secret Agent

#35 A Very Merry Christmas

#36 Geronimo's Valentine

#37 The Race Across America

#38 A Fabumouse School Adventure

#39 Singing Sensation

#40 The Karate Mouse

#41 Mighty Mount Kilimanjaro

#42 The Peculiar Pumpkin Thief

#43 I'm Not a Supermouse!

#44 The Giant Diamond Robbery

#45 Save the White Whale!

#46 The Haunted Castle

#47 Run for the Hills, Geronimo!

#48 The Mystery in Venice

#49 The Way of the Samurai

#50 This Hotel Is Haunted

#51 The Enormouse Pearl Heist

#52 Mouse in Space!

#53 Rumble in the Jungle

#54 Get into Gear, Stilton!

#55 The Golden Statue Plot